CRIME SCENE

CSI Reilly Steel - Prequel

CASEY HILL

CSI REILLY STEEL SERIES

Author Page

CHAPTER ONE

Forty miles south of Washington, DC in Prince William County, Virginia is the small town of Quantico.

Bordered on one side by the Potomac River and on the remaining three sides by the Marine Corps base, Quantico is home to the FBI training center. Situated among lush forestry, the 547 acre property is where recruits run obstacle courses, engage in firearms training and participate in mock hostage and terrorist scenarios in Hogan's Alley, the FBI's "real world" training town.

It was the world Reilly Steel was born for.

That was her first thought when she'd arrived at the Academy.

As she stepped off the bus one bright spring morning, she breathed in the fresh, crisp air. The next twenty weeks or so would make or break her and as far as she was concerned she'd already been broken plenty of times.

Now it was time to be remade.

In her 27 years, Reilly had seen more misery and faced more challenges than most people twice her age. Hardened and determined, she knew she was ready for whatever challenges awaited her on the other side of the guard shack.

Hoisting her purse onto her shoulder, and her suitcase rolling behind her, she strode up to the entrance gate.

"Reilly Steel reporting for training, sir," she said. The guard, whose name tag read 'Owens' glanced at her and realizing she was actually being polite and not snide like some of the other newbies, he gave her a small nod.

"Identification and acceptance letter please," he requested, holding out his hand. Reilly took the documents from her purse and handed them to him.

Owens looked over the documents, returned them to Reilly and released the gate. "Welcome to Quantico and the FBI training center," he'd said. Then pausing a moment, he added, "I hope you stick around."

Reilly glanced at him but could not discern whether he was being sarcastic or sincere. A tall, blonde-haired and blue-eyed Californian, she was used to snide comments from people who doubted her abilities based solely on her appearance.

Shrugging it off in any case, she thanked Owens and entered the grounds.

SHE ARRIVED at the dorm room listed on her registration papers and found it already occupied. The woman looked to be about Reilly's age, with thick auburn-red hair cut in a bob, wide green eyes, and a spate of freckles across her nose.

"Hi!" she chirped animatedly. "You must be Reilly. I'm Faye Williamson."

"Nice to meet you."

The two roommates began unpacking, rearranging the room and getting to know one another.

Both were from California, but from different areas; Reilly grew up in San Francisco, while Faye resided in Roseville near Sacramento. Reilly came from a working-class background while Faye's family was decidedly affluent.

Despite their differences, both women sensed that a true friendship had begun. Though Reilly was surprised at how open and forthcoming Faye was about her family, background and pretty much anything else they talked about.

A naturally reticent person by nature, she was taken aback by Faye's willingness to reveal absolutely everything there was to know about her — in the space of about a half hour. Reilly wondered if such a tendency would help or hinder her new friend in their future career.

Typically for her own part, she didn't reveal all that much about herself or her own background, save for the fact that she lived with her father in Marin County, had one sister and her mother was deceased.

Simple straightforward facts, yet hiding a world of complications.

THE TWO SPENT the remainder of the day walking the grounds and familiarizing themselves with the facility. "This place is so huge," commented Faye. "If we weren't in shape when we got here, we will be just from walking around campus."

Reilly had to agree; she'd known Quantico was massive, but now she was actually on the grounds, the training facility seemed larger than life.

Eventually, they decided to go back to their room and relax. "We might as well take a load off while we can," commented Faye. "Tomorrow is our first official day of training, and I have a feeling it's going to be a bear."

CHAPTER TWO

"Welcome to the FBI Training Center, and your first introduction to forensic analysis," Special Supervisory Agent Rob Crichton greeted the new recruits the following morning.

A tall, athletic looking man who looked to be in his late-forties with sandy-colored hair and weather-beaten skin, Crichton had a stern face but Reilly thought, the faint twinkle in his eye suggested he sounded a lot tougher than he actually was. "Over the next few weeks, we'll be spending quite a bit of time together."

Everyone in the room was attentive: all were facing forward, FBI-issue pens in hands and corresponding blank notebooks on desks, all of the students wearing identical blue polo shirts and khaki pants.

A few looked nervous. Most looked excited.

"Now," continued SSA Crichton, "you've all had a chance to get settled in, yes?" He paused, scanned the room for signs of agreement then continued, "Good. If not, you'd better, because if you haven't figured it out already, free time is not something agents in training have a lot of." Several students chuckled.

"Since today is your first day," he continued, "some of you may think we'll take it easy on you. Not a chance. We make you hit the ground running around here, and for good reason. The bad guys don't wait around until we feel up to catching them."

More chuckles and nods of agreement. "You all know about Hogan's Alley?" he ventured. More nods. "Excellent. We'll be hitting there sometime this week. We're not going to tell you when, or what the scenario will be, just be ready."

Reilly was grinning like a Cheshire cat. Secretly, she wished they were going to Hogan's Alley right now. She'd heard all about the legendary venue and the real-life situations acted out in the FBI's own mock town.

"Founded" in 1987 and located on over 10 acres of Academy grounds, most of the town's structures were classrooms, offices or facades, a bank (which was robbed frequently), a hotel, mayor's office, post office, a used car lot (whose cars aren't really for sale), and several homes and businesses — complete with a deli that did actually serve sandwiches.

It was for all intents and purposes, a functioning town, though populated by actors whose job it was to generally be as uncooperative as possible, thus testing trainee's abilities in a worst case scenario.

To Reilly, this sounded like a lot of fun.

LATER THAT DAY, the recruits changed into running attire and met on the running track. They were soon joined by another class.

As the two groups began pre-run stretching exercises, Faye whispered to Reilly, "It looks like all the really cute guys are in the other class. Check out that hottie over there, about three o'clock."

She glanced over and saw a tall, muscular, guy who looked to be about thirty years old. He noticed the two women looking at him, and instantly puffed up like a proud pigeon. Reilly rolled her eyes and whispered, "Not my type. Too self-absorbed."

"How can you tell from here?" Faye asked, mystified. "I think he's very cute."

The coach's whistle shrilled and he shouted for them all to line up on the track. Then his whistle sounded again, and the students began to run.

Not surprisingly, the tall guy Faye was interested in took off like a gazelle, pumping his long legs and quickly pulling ahead of the crowd.

Reilly paced herself, knowing that putting out a lot of energy at the start of the five mile run would leave her too depleted by the final laps. She watched Faye's "hottie" round the first corner and wondered how long before he lost his advantage and began to tire and fall behind.

She was surprised. He kept up a good pace for quite some time before grudgingly slowing, and even then finished his five miles before the majority of the other students. Any sliver of admiration Reilly might have felt was quickly extinguished however, when she watched him smirk and saunter off the field, scanning to see which girls were watching him as he strode away.

She resolved to find out who he was, for the sole purpose of avoiding him in the future.

Faye caught up with her after the run. "Dang, he's fast," she exclaimed. "Impressive run. I need to find out his name."

Reilly sighed. "What you need is to forget about guys and focus."

"Come on, it's our first day. Of course I'm going to check out the guys! Aren't you? Heck, we have to have some entertainment during the day."

"Precisely," Reilly replied, indicating their surroundings. "Surely being part of all this is entertainment enough. Forget the guys, they'll still be around when the training is done."

Faye laughed and shook her head. "I swear I am going to get you to go on a date if it's the last thing I do."

"Good luck with that," Reilly shot back, smiling.

There was some heavy competition — she was already in love with Quantico.

CHAPTER THREE

A t dinner that evening, SSA Rob Crichton came into the cafeteria.

Addressing the new recruits, he said, "I know we've given you a lot today, but we've got one more thing before you're off duty." A few groaned. "Hey, get used to it," he continued. "Twelve hour days are the norm here. Besides, I think you'll like this assignment. We're going to check out VirtSim."

Reilly heard several other students let out whoops of joy.

The Academy's VirtSim was a unique and coveted piece of law enforcement training equipment, developed specifically for the FBI.

"I see several of you are already familiar with this tool. In case you aren't, I'll explain briefly. VirtSim stands for Virtual Reality Tactical Training Simulator. It's a three-dimensional simulator that uses motion capture technology to record a participant's full body motion in a virtual 360-degree tactical environment. In other words, the environment will look and feel real to you. There will be avatars representing good guys or bad guys, what we call 'friendlies' or 'hostiles.'" He smirked a little. "Obviously the goal is to shoot the hostiles and not the friendlies."

TEN MINUTES LATER, the new recruits stood in the VirtSim room.

"As you can see, there's not much to this room," said Crichton. "That's because it's not the room that's important. It's the technology, and if you've never done a 360-degree virtual reality simulation before, this is going to blow your mind. I'd like to introduce you to one of our assistant instructors," he continued.

Turning slightly to his right, he indicated a man who stepped forward. Reilly heard Faye draw in a sharp breath; the guy was none other than the arrogant "hottie" from the running track.

"This is Jake Callahan, assistant instructor for VirtSim." He paused, then continued, "Jake is here because he's one of the most accurate and fastest students in VirtSim, so he's highly qualified to show you how to maneuver in the simulation. Remember, this is *virtual* reality, so it feels a bit different from the real world, even if it looks like it. Okay, Jake, take them in."

Jake stepped forward. "Thanks for the intro," he said with a smug smile.

Reilly was really beginning to really dislike the guy. She

glanced at Faye, who was staring at Jake as though he was golden. She rolled her eyes and returned her attention to the obnoxious older recruit.

"Okay, so what's going to happen is this: we're going to get you guys into the VR gear. When the simulation starts, you'll be in the chosen scenario with both hostiles and friendlies. The goal is to shoot the hostiles and protect the friendlies and your fellow agents.

The scenario we're using tonight will be the shopping mall. A gunman is loose in the mall, and it's our job to take him down without killing any shoppers or store employees. Okay, let's get rolling."

CHAPTER FOUR

The students put on the gear, and the simulation began.

Reilly was surprised at how very real, and at the same time surreal the simulation felt.

Looking down at her hands, they seemed strangely far away as though they belonged to someone else, yet still felt very much a part of her.

In the earpiece, she heard Jake say, "Okay, before the actual scenario starts, we're going to take a few minutes just to move around, so you can get the idea of how it feels when you maneuver." The students began to walk around, flexing their extremities, pulling out their "weapons," walking, jogging and touching objects in the simulation.

Reilly was surprised when she reached out to touch a fern in one of the pots of greenery in the center of the 'mall' and felt the edges of the leaves, just as real as the ones her mom had planted on their patio back home.

She briefly reflected that those same patio plants would likely be dead by the time she finished training; Reilly was the only one who remembered to care for them, and her father seldom had visitors or even ventured out there except to smoke.

Despite all his other bad habits, Mike Steel refused to smoke in the house because he disliked the stale smell.

It made her momentarily sad; in a way those plants were about the only thing in the house that had survived her mother's passing.

She shook off the thought and continued to explore the virtual world. After a few more minutes, she heard Jake's voice say, "Okay, get ready. Here we go."

Suddenly, the empty mall filled with people. Shoppers of all ages milled about, unaware of the impending danger. Reilly stood ready, knowing shots would ring out soon.

She didn't have long to wait. Automatic gunfire erupted from the upper level of the mall. People screamed and began running around. Some hit the floor, covering their heads. Many headed for the exits.

Reilly pushed her way through the crowd, heading for the escalator and the upper level. Scanning the tiers above her head, she tried to locate the gunman. It was difficult, as the shifting sea of people kept jostling her and cutting across her line of sight.

She deftly avoided them, focused on the upper level, and continued to scan for the shooter as she leaped up the escalator stairs, taking them two at a time and not waiting for the mechanism.

Skidding behind a door display in front of a department

store, she heard another burst of gunfire, more screams, and a man's voice yelling, "I'm gonna kill all of you. Damn idiot consumers. You're gonna all die now, you greedy sons of bitches."

Another burst of gunfire and more screams. Reilly peered cautiously around the display. She saw the gunman, about 20 yards away, standing near the railing of the second level near a health food store. Looking around for her fellow recruits, she noted that several of them had also made it to the second level and had eyes on the gunman.

Shoppers and store employees continued to pour out of the various shops, trying to be as unobtrusive as possible to avoid the shooter's attention. But the gunman heard the activity behind him, whirled around, and grabbed a woman as she tried to run away. She screamed as he grabbed her by her white coat (Reilly assumed she was a cosmetics sales person from a nearby makeup boutique), pulled her in front of him, and waved the gun in the air.

"This bitch is gonna die if you all don't back off," he snarled. Reilly made eye contact with the recruit nearest her, a guy named Jason, and indicated she intended to rush the gunman from behind and that he should cover her. Looking at her fellow recruits who had also made it to the second level, she made eye contact, communicated her plans with signals, received nods of agreement, and prepared to act.

Reilly crept from behind the display, moving low and slowly along the wall, crossing doorways as quickly as possible and taking shelter behind signs and displays as she went. So far, so good. The gunman hadn't noticed her movements. Cautiously, she made for the next object that could provide cover – a large cement pot containing more forestry and ferns.

Suddenly, there was a crash. The gunman spun around, looking for the source of the noise. As he scanned the area, his eyes lit on Reilly, who dove for cover, but not quite soon enough. The gunman caught the movement out of the corner of his eye. He spun towards Reilly and leveled his weapon at her.

She froze, then took a chance. Diving for the nearest open doorway she rolled to the side as the gunman fired.

She heard the ping of bullets near her head, and instinctively hunkered down. Her heart was pounding a million miles an hour; her ears rang with the sound of gunfire.

Reilly heard the gunman curse and let loose another burst of bullets in an arc surrounding him. A customer appearing from a nearby doorway made a break for the escalator.

The shooter turned and fired. The woman went down.

CHAPTER FIVE

Despite knowing this was a simulation, Reilly felt ill at the woman's demise.

Her heart still racing, she tried to determine the best course of action.

Peering out again from behind her makeshift cover, she looked for her fellow agents. Nearly all of them were up on the second level now; Reilly imagined a few were still on the lower level, guarding any escalators and stairwells the perpetrator might use for escape.

She tried to make eye contact again with Jason, but his attention was elsewhere, and she didn't want to make any sound that might draw the gunman's eye.

He was still standing near the railing, holding the hysterical woman in front of him, and waving the gun around.

He looked crazed; his hair was disheveled, and even from a distance, you could see the dark circles under his eyes. His skin tone was waxy and dull, and his teeth were nearly black. Drug addict, thought Reilly. Most likely meth.

That meant he was irrational and likely had no plan, other than to obtain money or drugs, or money for drugs.

She assumed he must work for a dealer or other drug kingpin; your garden-variety meth user, she reasoned, would probably not have access to an automatic weapon or the incredible amount of ammunition he was burning through. Every few seconds, he'd shout out more obscenities and threats and fire his weapon randomly into the now-deserted mall.

In her earpiece, Reilly heard Jake issuing instructions. "Okay rookies," he said, "enough hiding behind stuff. Get your butts out there and take this guy down. You need to confront him, people."

Reilly looked toward her fellow recruits. Everyone exchanged glances.

Then Hillary, a tall brunette, motioned for Jason and Reilly to cover her while she rushed the gunman from behind. All nodded in agreement and got ready to move. Again, Reilly heard Jake barking into their earpieces. "Come on, what are you waiting for? Rush him."

Irritated, she turned her focus back to Jason and Hillary. Jake's ill-timed instruction had thrown off their timing. Instead of rushing forward as planned, Hillary froze.

The gunman turned and saw her frozen mid-step. He leveled his weapon at her. There was no time for Hillary to move out of harm's way, and both Jason and Reilly were too far away to intercept.

Suddenly, out of another shop doorway further down the mall, Jake burst out, holding an automatic weapon of his own. With a primal scream, he ran straight for the gunman, firing continuously. The hostage was hit first; she crumpled to the ground and the gunman was riddled with bullets.

As the echo of gunfire died away, she heard Rob Crichton's voice in their ear buds. "Okay, that's it. Let's get out."

CHAPTER SIX

The virtual reality faded away, giving over to the reality of the nearly empty VirtSim room.

"And that, ladies and gentlemen, was an excellent demonstration of how we do *not* resolve a conflict," Crichton said tightly.

"Yeah well, it was taking too long," said Jake. "Maybe next time they'll get to it faster."

Rob glared at him. "The point is not how long it takes," he said tersely. "The point is to *not* kill the hostage while the *agents* get the gunman." Turning to the rest of the class, he said, "You'll have to excuse our somewhat over-zealous instructor. Now go get some sleep. Tomorrow's another long one, and we'll be trying the VirtSim again. Preferably without the heroics next time." And with that, he turned and left the room.

Reilly wanted nothing more than to follow SSA Crichton's advice. She was tired, and frustrated with their first

VirtSim run. If only that idiot Jake hadn't gotten so impatient, and spoken up at the wrong time. . .

Faye was saying something to her, but she was lost in her own thoughts. She turned to ask her friend to repeat her comments — and found herself face to face with Jake.

"Hey there," he said in an oily tone that Reilly supposed was meant to be sexy but only sounded creepy. She gave him a small, insincere smile and tried to step around him, but he moved to block her way.

"So were you impressed?" he asked her. Reilly almost shot back a harsh reply, then checked herself. Instead of telling him what a colossal idiot she thought he was, she merely said, "It was definitely interesting."

"Yeah. Always feels great when you've saved the universe." He laughed like he really thought his comment was funny.

"Yes, it was something all right ..." Reilly bit her tongue.

"I always like to wind down after I off somebody in VirtSim," Jake continued. "How about we go get a beer and get to know one another better?"

She forced herself to keep her tone even, wishing she could wipe the smirk off his face with the back of her hand. "I'm tired. I need to get some rest," she said. Moving past him, she started for the door.

"I'll take you up on that beer," Reilly heard Faye say.

Jake gave her a look. "I was asking *her*."

Faye flushed but didn't say a word. She merely picked up her gear and followed Reilly out of the room.

"I can't believe he just said that to me," she raged. "I'm

going to get him to take me out if it takes all 20 weeks."

"And I can't believe you still want to, especially after what he just said," replied Reilly open-mouthed. "Faye, he's a jerk. You deserve better than that."

"Maybe, but I want *him*."

Reilly shook her head, mystified. "Just be careful what you wish for."

BACK IN THE ROOM, the two began to prepare for bed.

"Boy, am I beat," Reilly yawned. "I know it was a busy day, but I am extra-tired for some reason."

"Probably the nightmare," Faye said simply

Reilly's head snapped up. "What? What nightmare?"

"Last night about 2 am, you woke me up. You were whimpering in your sleep. Then you started talking but I couldn't understand what you were saying. It sounded like you were pleading with someone. Then you screamed. I tried to wake you, but I couldn't. You calmed down though, so I figured you were okay. You scared the holy crap out of me, though. What were you dreaming about?"

"I . . . don't remember," Reilly replied, her cheeks coloring.

Damn.

Luckily, Faye decided not to press for an explanation and although Reilly genuinely didn't remember having the nightmare, she knew well what the dream was about.

It was the same one she'd been having every night since her mother was murdered.

So much for being remade.

CHAPTER SEVEN

The following day, the recruits were taken outside to a mock crime scene in a wooded area on campus. Rob Crichton informed them that the purpose of the exercise was to process the crime scene and form a hypothesis on what had occurred.

The students were to examine the scene on their own, make notes and come together after one hour to discuss their findings. Crichton would then critique their observations and hypotheses, filling in any missing information.

Reilly and her fellow recruits began to study the mock crime scene. Near a large tree, there was a man's baseball cap in the dirt and beside it, a torn shirt with blood stains, and a small, bloody pocketknife.

The students were instructed to examine the evidence for 30 minutes without touching anything. She immediately noted that the baseball cap, a faded blue color with no logo, was upside down. The shirt, a cheap white tank top known as a "wife beater," was torn at the shoulder as though someone had pulled on it.

The blood stains, few but large, were surrounding a slash about chest level. The pocket knife, a keychain-sized model, lay with its tiny blade open on the ground, covered in blood to the handle. The knife was blue in color and the small ring at the end, usually attached to a larger key ring, was empty.

No keys were in sight. There were no marks on the tree itself, but there were signs of a scuffle in the dirt surrounding the roots. Unfortunately no distinct footprints or patterns were visible though, as the dirt area gave way to grass within a few feet of the base of the tree. The grass however, was quite smashed and compacted with signs of an escalating struggle. Reilly carefully examined the ground and found what she guessed she was supposed to be looking for — a small puddle of blood amidst the disturbed grass.

When 30 minutes had elapsed, SSA Crichton removed the crime scene tape and allowed the students to examine the evidence more closely. Reilly went straight for the knife. Pulling on her latex gloves, she picked it up and began to look at it more closely.

The blood on the knife stopped right before the blade ended and the casing began, which could mean that the attacker's hand had slid up the knife as he stabbed. She turned it over and noted that the typical logo displayed on the case of such blades had been covered with a small rose decal.

Relinquishing the blade to one of her fellow recruits,

Reilly moved on to the shirt. Several students were already examining it, so she patiently waited for them to finish. In the meantime, she observed the others present.

Faye was paired with Jason Bretherton, a handsome man of 32 from the Louisiana Bayou. He had light brown hair and hazel eyes, a somewhat heavy "Loo-ziana" accent, a broad chest, and an even broader smile.

Despite his charming accent and friendly openness, Jason impressed Reilly as a perceptive, contemplative man. She watched him now as he and Faye examined the base-ball cap. Jason was flirting and Faye was flirting back. Reilly was glad; maybe she would forget about that annoying Jake Callahan.

She then turned her attention to the trio examining the shirt: Jordan Nance, a highly intelligent computer geek from Detroit; Michael Wayne Bolton, (and yes, he'd heard all the jokes about his name, which is why he insisted they call him Butch), a Mormon and former Sheriff from Missouri; and Farhad Azizi, a graphic novelist from New York City.

The three seemed to be engrossed in the blood stain pattern. Reilly continued to observe, allowing her eyes to play over the scene, looking for any further clues. Seeing nothing, she moved closer to the three guys. They greeted her, indicated they were finished with the shirt, passed it to her, and moved on.

Reilly looked over the shirt, noting the blood stain pattern and examining the tear. Someone had definitely gripped this man's shirt tightly, ripping the fabric and pulling it off his body. She detected a faint aroma; slightly flowery with an undertone of musk. She sniffed the shirt more closely, searching for the source of the scent.

As she neared the torn shoulder, the smell intensified slightly. Reilly inhaled it again, then moved on to see if the scent was elsewhere. Coming to the opposite shoulder of the shirt, she detected it again. Following the scent down the shirt toward the blood stain, she tracked to where the smell of the "blood" (Reilly detected no metallic odor, so she knew it had to be stage blood) interfered with the flowery-musky scent. Turning the shirt over, she smelled the back of the garment. The smell was present but only faintly. She guessed this was due to the time the garment had spent lying on the ground — the smell had transferred from the front of the shirt to the back.

Reilly bent down to where it had been lying. At first she saw nothing but trampled dirt and grass. But as she looked more closely, she noticed a tiny spot of color — something tiny and bright pink. Picking up the object with a tweezers, she discovered it was the tip of a painted fingernail. She'd nearly missed it; it had been hidden mostly under the edge of the grass where it stopped and gave way to the dirt surrounding the tree.

Laura and Nicole Stewart from Seattle, twin sisters with jet black hair and dark eyes, approached and asked if they could examine the shirt. Reilly handed it to them, but kept the discovery of the fingernail to herself.

When the twins bent to examine the shirt, she replaced the fingernail where she'd found it.

Interesting....

CHAPTER EIGHT

After 15 minutes of examination, the students gathered together near the "crime scene." SSA Crichton queried what the evidence had told them, and what they thought happened.

A few scenarios, including a drug deal gone bad, a mugging, and a variation of Reilly's own suspicions (albeit missing a few key pieces of evidence) were proposed, but Crichton gave no indication which scenario, if any was correct. When it came time for Reilly to speak, she proposed her theory — the scene indicated an unsuccessful rape attempt and the wrath of the intended victim on the perpetrator.

"And how did you come to that conclusion?" asked Crichton, his expression giving nothing away.

"Well, at first I thought it was an attempted robbery too, but when I found the fingernail and smelled the perfume . . ."

"Excuse me?" Crichton interrupted. "Did you say you smelled perfume?"

She paused, wondering if she'd come to the wrong conclusion somehow, but it was the best theory she had, so she proceeded. "Yes, at least I think it was perfume. It was flowery and sweet, so I assumed it was a woman's. I didn't get enough to maybe pinpoint the brand so I'm only guessing, but it didn't smell like a man's cologne. Too feminine."

"I see. And you also mentioned a fingernail?"

"Yes, there was the tip of a woman's fingernail, painted bright pink, right at the edge of the grass and the dirt, under the tank top. I almost missed it at first but when I bent down and took a closer look . . . "

"So what do you think happened, Steel?"

"I think that our 'victim' was actually a perpetrator who got what he deserved. He accosted a woman, pulled her close to him and told her he was going to rape her. And she retaliated by fighting back. She had a small pocket knife, which she managed to get out of her purse or pocket and use it to stab him, but the wound would have been fairly superficial because she lacked the strength to jam the blade in all the way. I could tell by where the blood ended on the blade. I mean, it could have been that her hand slipped, but that would be more likely if the attacker was another man. He likely slapped her hand away or something right after she stabbed him. She freaked out because the wound bled a lot at first, and that made him angry too, so I'm guessing she fled and he attempted to chase her. But she must have gotten away or someone else showed up and spooked him, because after the signs of the struggle near the tree, there aren't any more patches like that on the grass nearby."

Crichton's face was impassive. "Congratulations. You've just solved the case."

After class, he called Reilly over. "Do you mean to tell me that you could actually smell the perfume on the shirt?"

She paused. "Yes, sir," she replied cautiously.

"Incredible," the instructor said, with faint admiration in his tone. "No one ever got the perfume clue, so we gave up putting it on the shirt. Over 8 months ago."

CHAPTER NINE

The remainder of the first week was extremely busy and long.

Each day's activities lasted 12 hours or longer, and by Friday evening the recruits were dragging. Everyone wanted a break but was too tired to do anything about it.

Saturday was a different story. They had the weekends off, which as training progressed would evolve into much-needed extra study and sleep time.

This first weekend however was another story. Nearly all the recruits were eager to blow off some steam.

About 1:00 Saturday afternoon, rumors began circulating about an off-campus party that night.

The location was an absent relative's home of a friend of one of new recruits. The address was passed around. The party would begin at 7 pm. There would be booze.

By 6:30 that evening, nearly everyone had left campus for the party. Faye and Reilly were still getting dressed.

Faye kept changing her clothes, insisting that she looked terrible in everything, eventually settling on a little black dress, patterned tights, and high-heeled boots.

Reilly kept it low-key with a simple white T-shirt, jeans and boots. By 7:00, they were ready to go. Both were looking forward to the evening. The weather was perfect, and they felt they could use a change of scenery, since they hadn't left the FBI compound all week.

As they were leaving Faye said, "I really hate to be late, but I think we need to grab a bite to eat before we go. I have a feeling I may drink a little tonight, so I need some ballast before I start." Seeing Reilly's startled look, she hastened to add, "Don't worry, I won't be driving us home. You can drive a stick shift, right?"

"Absolutely." Reilly wasn't much of a drinker, so she didn't mind being designated driver. Secretly, she had been itching to drive Faye's car. It was a classic, and had a 420cc engine that tore up the road. She had a weakness for fast, powerful automobiles — particularly muscle cars and Faye's was a classic '67 Mustang convertible in Nightmist Blue that she and her brother had restored several years before. Original interior and upholstery, the car had been flawless but missing the engine.

Faye explained that her brother had bought it from an elderly woman whose husband had passed away the year before. The car had been in the garage for at least two decades.

He'd wanted to teach her about cars so "no slime ball

mechanic can pull one over on my little sister." It had been a valuable education, and more fun than Faye could have imagined.

THE TWO WENT to a Mexican restaurant near the Quantico compound. When Reilly had time to relax she loved to cook, particularly Cajun and Mexican dishes. She made a mean chile relleno, if she said so herself.

The restaurant wasn't busy but the service was slow, so Reilly and Faye didn't finish eating until nearly 8:00. Undeterred, they headed for the party.

The festivities were taking place at a house in the nearby hills; Reilly had checked the directions online and printed them out and as Faye had a GPS device, they were confident they wouldn't be too late.

But after driving around for over half an hour, repeatedly losing the GPS signal and finding errors in the online map, they had to admit they were lost.

Frustrated, they pulled over. Taking some time to get their bearings and discerning where they were based on their previous wanderings, they decided on a direction and set out again. The GPS came back on intermittently and using the internet map, what information came from the GPS, as well as their instincts, they eventually found the party.

So much for sharp instincts, Reilly thought darkly.

CHAPTER TEN

B y the time they parked the Mustang, it was nearly 9:00.

Getting out of the car, Reilly and Faye headed for the house. They'd had to park near the far end of the street, and Faye was now loudly bemoaning her choice of footwear.

As they approached the property, Reilly noticed how quiet it seemed. It certainly looked like a gathering was taking place — every available parking spot had been taken, including several cars parked on the lawn. It was obvious the yard had been well-manicured, but now it sported deep gouges in the lawn from partygoers using it as a parking lot.

Faye didn't comment on the cars on the lawn, but she did say, "Doesn't it seem a little quiet for a party?"

"I was just noticing that," Reilly replied. "Obviously, it's a full house from all the cars parked here, but I don't hear any people. What could be going on?"

"I hope we didn't blow it and miss the whole thing," Faye exclaimed. "Jake is supposed to be here tonight."

"For Chris-sakes Faye, get over that guy. He's an ass. In fact now that I know he's supposed to be here maybe I'll just wait in the car," she added wickedly.

"Oh come on. There will be plenty of other guys there too. We went through hell to get here. Let's just go inside and see what's going on. Besides, I seriously need a beer."

The two walked up the driveway and to the front door. It stood open, so they walked in.

Listening for a moment, they realized they could hear voices now. They all seemed to be coming from the back yard, but far from revelers in the throes of a big celebration, they didn't sound happy. In fact, it sounded as though people were arguing. Reilly thought she could also hear a few women crying.

Giving each other questioning looks, they followed the sounds.

As Reilly and Faye stepped through the back door onto the patio, they both pulled up short, nearly knocking each other over in the process.

A few yards away on the ground was the body of a man, blood on his head and on the concrete paving beneath him and surrounded by about 40 partygoers, who were all in a complete panic.

Reilly looked over at Faye, who had gone pale. Now that they were amongst the drunk and terrified partygoers, they could hear what was being said, but couldn't identify the individual speakers. Bits of conversation drifted their way.

"This is so bad man, we are all gonna get kicked out of the Academy . . . "

"What are we supposed to do now? We can't call the freakin' cops!"

"We gotta do something! Are you sure he's dead?"

"Of course he's dead, you moron. His head is bashed open."

"Well, did anybody check his pulse?"

"Oh, are *you* gonna go and check, Mr. Tough Guy? I'm not getting blood on me and implicating *my*self."

"Hey, don't talk that way to me!"

"What's wrong with you people? We have got to call the cops!"

"Hell no, I'm not even supposed to be here. I can't be involved in this."

"Oh my god, oh my god, oh my GOD! We can't call the cops or we'll all go to jail! We gotta jam.... I gotta jam...."

"Nobody's going anywhere until we get rid of this body."

The partygoers erupted anew in argument, some in favor and some opposed to covering up the incident.

Reilly glanced around and noticing a nearby picnic table, she jumped up on it.

"Hey!" she yelled at the top of her voice. The entire group went silent.

"First of all," she continued, "no one is touching or moving anything, including themselves." She caught movement out of the corner of her eye and pointed at a blond woman trying to sneak out. "Don't even think about it. Each and every one of us is staying right here. No one is touching anything. In fact, we need to clear this area."

"Oh Reilly," Faye implored, "Let's just get out of here. We didn't have anything to do with this."

"Precisely," Reilly replied, "so, we have nothing to worry about. Faye, please do the honors."

"Huh?" Her friend was baffled, but for Reilly, the next move was obvious.

"Call Nine One One. *Now*. This is a crime scene."

CHAPTER ELEVEN

F aye again opened her mouth to protest, but catching a look from Reilly, thought better of it and reached for her cell phone. Noting the weak signal, she headed inside to use a land line.

Meanwhile, the other partygoers were beginning to reawaken from the temporarily stunned state her command had caused. Noticing this, she took charge of the group again.

"Don't even think about leaving," she ordered. "Every single one of you is going in to the house, right now. You're all material witnesses. Man I shouldn't have to be telling you this. Most of you are in the Academy. You should be ashamed of yourselves. Go inside, find the first available seat, and stay there until the police arrive. When they do, you will all cooperate in an orderly fashion. Understood?" Stunned into silence once again, the group merely nodded, but no one moved.

"Are you deaf?" Reilly urged. "Move it."

Slowly, as if they were extras in a George Romero zombie classic, the now-sober partiers moved as one into the house.

Once they'd situated themselves inside, and Faye informed everyone (in a shaky voice) that the police were on their way, Reilly again addressed them.

"Okay who's in charge of this party?" she asked.

A hand from a small cluster seated on the large sectional sofa tentatively went up. Reilly recognized the young man, but she only knew his first name – Terry. From her observations of him in class, he seemed a bit unfocused and his performance mediocre. She'd wondered how he'd made it into the Academy.

"What's your name?" Reilly asked.

"Terry. Terry Nordingham," the young man replied.

"Okay Terry, tell me what happened here."

"I ...I wasn't there. I came up on the whole thing when people started screaming and shouting."

"Okay then, who was first on the scene?"

Silence.

"Come off it, folks — it's just us here now. If you think I'm being pushy, wait for a few minutes until the authorities get here. You'd better get used to explaining what happened, because we're all about to do a whole lot of that. So out with it — who was first on the scene?"

For some reason, Reilly wasn't surprised when Jake Callahan slowly got up from a chair in an adjoining room. She heard Faye gasp.

"I went to use the master bathroom upstairs because

some chick was puking in the downstairs one," Jake began, his voice slurred and his movements unsteady. Clearly he was drunk. "When I came out, there were these two guys arguing in the bedroom by the window. One pushed the other, then they started shoving and punching, so I got the hell out of there. As I reach the bottom of the stairs, I hear a thud outside, so I run out, and one of the dudes is on the ground bleeding. So I yelled for help."

"Do you see the other man here now?" asked Reilly.

Jake looked around briefly, then lazily shook his head. "Nope."

Reilly was irritated. OK, so he was drunk but couldn't the guy quit the attitude for even one second, given what had just happened? A man had just died for Christ's sake.

"What did he look like?"

"I didn't get a good look at either of them, actually."

"So how can you be sure he's not here?"

Jake sighed. "'Cos I know most of the people here. I'm looking around, and I see familiar faces. This guy's face was not familiar. Ergo he's not here."

"Did anyone else see anything?" Reilly asked tersely, turning her attention away from Jake. No one spoke; and many people shook their heads.

Just then, the group heard the sound of approaching sirens.

The police and paramedics had arrived.

CHAPTER TWELVE

"Five-oh in the house," someone muttered.

"Okay take out your IDs and get ready to cooperate," Reilly commanded. "And clear a path for the EMT's."

Scanning the room for any fellow recruits, she noted who was there – Faye of course; as well as Hillary Bogdonovich and the dark-haired Stewart twins, who were huddled together in a corner, looking stunned.

Southern Gentleman Jason Bretherton; fellow classmates Farhad Azizi and Jordan Nance; and a few others Reilly recognized on sight but whose names she couldn't immediately recall. She also recognized a few others from the academy who were in different classes than hers – Jake Callahan of course, but also individuals she'd only seen around the compound.

There were perhaps a dozen or so that Reilly did not recognize; most likely they were just locals, not FBI

recruits. Not surprisingly, "Butch" Bolton was not in atten-
dance. As a devout Mormon, Butch did not drink. *He'll be
especially happy he missed this 'party,'* she thought.

Reilly met the police at the front door and briefly
explained what little she knew.

Faye must have told the 9-1-1 operator how many
people were present, because patrol cars containing 9 officers had arrived on the scene to interview witnesses, as
well as a fire department vehicle (who had arrived mere
seconds before the police) and an ambulance. Additionally,
two forensics from the CSI unit pulled up in a van to
photograph and process the evidence.

The lights from all the emergency vehicles lit up the
outside area in a dizzying spectacle of rotating red and blue
lights. Right then, Reilly was glad they'd been so late to the
party and that she'd only had one margarita with dinner
over an hour and a half ago, so now she was clear-headed
and sharp.

Faye joined her on the porch, and they began to relate
to one of the officers what little they had seen and heard.
As the women were relating their observations SSA Rob
Crichton pulled up.

Clearly, someone must have called him and alerted him
to the presence of so many Academy recruits at the party.
He screeched to a halt in the street right behind the mob
of police cars. Jogging toward the front walk, an officer
turned to stop him but then recognizing him, pointed the
way and let him by.

Reilly watched as SSA Crichton walked into the house
at a clipped pace. At first, she was certain he did not see

them but as he was almost through the front door, he stopped suddenly and turned, a puzzled expression on his face.

"I didn't expect to find you in such company, Ms. Steel," he said then noticing Faye, he nodded to her, by contrast not looking all that surprised to see her. "Ms. Williamson." Turning back to Reilly he asked, "Were you here when the incident occurred?"

She shook her head. "No. Faye and I were quite late to the ... festivities."

"In retrospect, how fortunate."

"We thought so too. We got lost on our way here, and we'd stopped for dinner too, so we arrived after everything had already gone down. All I know is there's a young man I don't recognize lying on the patio outside with a broken head, and when we got here everyone was freaking out. We tried to stop them from moving the body and further trampling the crime scene," she made a face, "but I think we were a little too late for that."

"I see. What happened next?"

Reilly continued outlining events as best she could in chronological fashion. "We asked them to come inside and sit down while Faye called the authorities."

"Asked?" Faye repeated, wide-eyed at this rather tame description. She took up the story. "Reilly questioned the partygoers and Jake Callahan stepped forward, sir. He said that he was in the bathroom in the master suite upstairs, and when he came out two men were arguing in the adjoining bedroom. According to Jake, a shoving match ensued, so he went downstairs to avoid getting involved.

As he arrived at the lower level, he heard a thud outside, went to investigate and found our victim on the ground, bleeding."

SSA Crichton glanced at Faye, his expression somewhat kinder this time "I see," he said. "Well, it's a good thing for everyone you two showed up when you did, because if anybody'd moved that body, every recruit here would have been expelled from the Academy. I would have seen to that personally." He gave them a brief nod, then continued, "Now if you'll please excuse me, I need to talk to Jake - find out what kind of trouble my idiot nephew has gotten into this time." Turning on his heel, SSA Crichton strode into the house.

Faye was open-mouthed. "*Nephew?* Jake is Crichton's nephew?"

"Seems that way." Reilly too had been struck by this unexpected development but thinking about how dismissive and cocky Jake had seemed towards their instructor during the VirtSim exercise earlier, now it made sense.

"Wow, am I glad I'm not Jake right now," Faye went on. "Crichton is sca-ry."

Reilly looked her. "So are you now over the fascination you had with that moronic, drunken fool whose own uncle describes him as an idiot?"

Faye's eyes took on a familiar dreamy look. "Not a chance."

CHAPTER THIRTEEN

R eilly and Faye were released from the scene almost immediately; it was clear to the investigating officers the two had nothing to do with the events at the party.

Both gave their contact information should the police wish to contact them again, so there was no need for them to stay. Faye wanted to go home, but Reilly insisted they stick around for a bit; she wanted to hear a broader explanation (for she was sure there was one) of what had happened. Faye complained but eventually gave in; she had to admit that Reilly was right when she'd pointed out that neither of them would be able to sleep after all that had occurred.

Faye's major complaint was her choice of footwear — her feet hurt from the high heels. Reilly resolved this by pointing out that Faye had her workout gear in the trunk of the car and could change into her tennis shoes, which her friend protested for fashion reasons. But eventually function won out over form, and Faye agreed to change into the more comfortable but fashion-backward shoes and accompany Reilly on her quest to discover what had transpired. She had to agree that Jake's explanation sounded too simplistic, even for him.

While they had been resolving Faye's footwear dilemma, several now-sober and tired partygoers had been cleared, and were headed for their vehicles.

A few who had not passed a breathalyzer test waited for a local cab company to send drivers; still others waited for rides from awakened parents, friends or significant others. Reilly and Faye were getting the shoes from the Mustang's trunk when they heard an angry outburst from the back patio area of the property. Curious, Reilly hurried toward the sound, leaving Faye behind to tie her shoes. Faye called after her, but Reilly didn't hear. She made her way through the huge living room and the gigantic open floor plan kitchen/family room area to the back patio. The crime scene now had a large area cordoned off with yellow police tape.

The EMTs had taken the victim's vitals and declared that he was indeed deceased.

SSA Crichton was standing near the edge of the tape, holding his nephew Jake firmly by the upper arm. Reilly saw fury on the agent's face, and some terror on Jake's. She froze in place; even though Crichton was not directing his attention towards her, the icy yet volatile anger he exuded chilled her to the bone. It reminded her of an expression she'd seen on her father's face many times. She fervently hoped that Crichton was better at controlling his temper than her father was.

As if reading her thoughts, SSA Crichton released his nephew's arm. Turning to the uniformed officer, he asked, "Are you finished with my nephew, Officer Mayridge? Or shall I leave him in your capable hands?"

Mayridge stepped forward, cleared his throat and said, "I believe we're done with him for now. As long as he stays in town and doesn't attend any more parties," here he shot Jake a sidelong glance, "we should be okay to release him. But he's a material witness so we may want to talk to him again, perhaps when he remembers more about the incident."

"No worries about any of that Terry," Rob replied, also shooting a glance at Jake, who shifted uncomfortably from foot to foot. "If my nephew here thought he'd been under my thumb before tonight, he's in for a big lesson in what surveillance really means."

Reilly almost felt sorry for Jake.

Almost.

SSA Crichton looked up then and seeing Reilly, he nodded a greeting. "Ms. Steel," he called out. "I thought you'd be gone home by now. Don't tell me Ms. Williamson wanted to stick around?"

"Not exactly," she replied. She paused then, realizing she was overstepping her bounds but curiosity was getting the better of her. "I'm sorry ...I guess I'm just interested to find out what exactly happened tonight. Though I know I'm probably in the way here, I should get going . . ."

"I have questions too and was thinking of taking a look

around myself, once the officials have finished." Jake gave his uncle a look of mild surprise but refrained from commenting. "Perhaps Officer Mayridge can give my errant nephew a ride home." The policeman nodded his assent and Crichton continued. "I'd like to take a look at a few things, maybe talk to a couple of the remaining witnesses." He looked at Reilly. "I wouldn't mind a second set of eyes and ears."

She was taken aback. He wanted her help? "I – I'd be honored," she stammered, and felt herself blush. Inwardly, she cursed this tendency to do when praised.

She'd heard kind words spoken about herself so rarely after her mother died, that she couldn't help it. And given that SSA Crichton was not only her tutor but such a highly respected crime scene investigator ... Reilly guessed there was a little hero-worship involved too.

Jake and Mayridge left in the patrol car, and feeling more excited than she cared to admit, Reilly went in search of Faye to tell her she was free to go and that SSA Crichton had agreed to give her a ride home. She didn't have far to look; Faye was lying on a large sectional couch in the living room, fast asleep. Reilly woke her, and after making sure she was awake, fully sober and capable of driving she bid her goodnight.

"Don't wait up. I have a feeling I'll be here for a few hours."

"You really do love this stuff, don't you?" said Faye. "Earlier when you were ordering everyone around, if I didn't know better I'd swear you were already a Fed."

Reilly nodded. "I guess I do. But it's not just that.

Somebody died tonight, and so far the answers aren't adding up."

Faye grinned at her new friend. "Spoken like a true investigator. Then get to it, and let me know what you find out."

CHAPTER FOURTEEN

Reilly found SSA Crichton behind the crime scene tape, wearing latex gloves, and kneeling carefully next to the body, examining the head wound.

As she approached, he looked up and she noted that he looked tired.

"Go ahead and step under the tape Ms. Steel," he directed. "CSI are finished here."

Reilly did so, saying, "Call me Reilly, please. 'Ms. Steel' feels so formal."

"All right Reilly," he replied. "And for convenience's sake, you can call me Rob."

It felt strange and somewhat disconcerting to be on first name terms with her tutor, but she wasn't going to argue.

"I want to show you something here." He offered Reilly a pair of latex gloves, which she took and put on. "See the blood there on the cement, and the wound on the victim's head?" He pointed with the end of a pen he'd pulled from his pocket. "Does anything about it look odd to you?"

"Has the body been moved? By the paramedics I mean."

"No, the ME hasn't arrived yet."

Reilly bent closer, resting carefully on one knee, and inspected the head wound, being careful not to touch the body. It matched the size and shape of the bloodstain on the ground and the amount of blood seemed appropriate for a head wound of that size. She looked closer, her instincts on high alert. Everything seemed correct for the circumstances, but yet something nagged at the back of her mind. She wrinkled her nose, thinking.

"What is it?" Rob asked.

"I'm not sure. You're right; something just seems — off somehow. I mean the size of the wound and the amount of blood appears consistent, but . . ."

She paused, and he picked up her thought, "But something about a young, strapping guy falling from a height of two stories and just dying instantly just doesn't wash."

"Exactly."

"I thought the same thing," he replied. "And then I thought okay, even if he was really drunk or on drugs or something, which we won't know until the tox screens come back, and whatever he'd ingested earlier caused him to die from the fall, why didn't any of the geniuses in the dining room hear anything? We need to talk to some of those people. Did they all clear out once the police were done with them?"

"I think so," she replied. "Want me to check if there's anyone left?"

"Let's both go and check. I want to see what the dining room looked like anyway."

They proceeded into the dining room, where a mess of empty bottles, shot glasses, a few soggy quarters and spilled alcohol awaited.

The two remaining officers originally on the scene and the just-arrived coroner were already there. Rob knew the coroner, Dr. Hendrickson only slightly, but had dealt with her before and knew her to be thorough and tenacious. He introduced Reilly and following Rob's queries, the officer informed them that all witnesses had been questioned and released.

"I want to check out the arrangement here," Rob told Reilly, when the others moved on. "Witnesses seem to consistently support the contention that the vast majority of the partygoers were in this room when Jake began shouting. There were what, about 35, 40 people here when you arrived?" She nodded and he continued, "So taking into account Jake himself, the person he said he heard throwing up in the bathroom, the victim, the guy who pushed him, and maybe a couple other people who were in another part of the house at the time ... let's estimate we've got about 30 or so people in here then." They looked around, visualizing that many individuals crowded around the large, banquet-sized dining table for a drinking game.

It was indeed possible that so many could have fit in this room, thought Reilly, albeit there would be a few who probably chose to stand. She counted 18 proper dining chairs, an overstuffed rectangular ottoman dragged in from the nearby living room, an expensive-looking leather office chair, and five barstools whose lone mate stood near the breakfast nook on the opposite side of the kitchen. That totaled 24; 25 if two slender people shared the footstool. There was at least one more barstool available for use, but it had been left behind at the breakfast nook. So, Reilly reasoned either not everyone was accounted for, or at least 5 people stood while the game was being played.

Rob spoke up then. "What are you thinking?" he asked and she told him what she'd deduced.

"I was considering something similar," he said. "Also, these guys aren't worried about getting colds or flu. There are only six glasses on this table — that's a whole lot of sharing. Guess they figured the alcohol would kill the germs." He barked a brief laugh. "Not really. One reason I didn't go in for games like this in college — all my buddies kept getting sick with colds and crap the week after every frat party. I stuck to having my own beer glass."

Reilly looked at the table, and wrinkled her nose "They were certainly drunk enough by the time I got here." Her stomach roiled at the stench of alcohol. It stank in here — not just of alcohol but also sweat, mixed with a particularly pungent male cologne. "Though they seem to have spilled as much as they drank," she added, noting the still-wet beer stains surrounding the table.

"I wonder if they spilled all that during the game, or whether they jarred the table when they heard Jake yell."

Reilly used her cellphone camera to snap several photos of the dining area, the party deitrus, the table itself and a vodka bottle — one of the few empties that was lying upright and not on its side, which struck her as curious.

CHAPTER FIFTEEN

She brought the bottle to her nose, and holding it by the neck, sniffed the bottom and sides.

She definitely detected vodka, which seemed to get stronger as she neared the neck.

That was strange, she thought; given that the bottle was upright, one would assume that any spilled liquid would have pooled at the bottom, creating a stronger smell in that area.

Inhaling again, Reilly moved her hands to the base and sniffed inside the bottle, but detected little or no odor there.

Puzzled, she moved away to the kitchen where there were no competing alcohol scents, though the cologne was still present there too.

Rob followed and watched as she stood the bottle on the countertop, put her hands behind her back, and inhaled the interior; once, twice, then a third time.

Turning to him she said, "There's an extremely weak alcohol smell in this, as though someone had poured out the contents, then briefly rinsed the inside and filled it again with water. The outside of the bottle has a stronger smell than the inside, suggesting some of the vodka splashed on it while it was being poured out. It should be the other way around."

"Nice observation, but how is it relevant?" he asked.

"I'm not sure. Like you said, it's just an observation." Feeling silly, she quickly returned the bottle to its original position alongside a crime scene marker on the floor.

Much to Reilly's relief (for the sake of her nose if nothing else), they then left the dining area and made their way upstairs towards the bedroom, and the balcony from which the victim fell.

She followed Crichton into the master suite. It certainly looked as though some kind of scuffle had occurred. A reading lamp had toppled from a small table, the chair beside it was overturned, and the draperies hung askew, as though they'd been pulled, perhaps by the victim to try and prevent a fall.

He and Reilly began to move around the room, although they weren't sure what they should be looking for. Other than a few objects overturned, a small table and a couple of books from the surrounding bookshelves, nothing stood out.

All of a sudden she realized how tired she was and was grateful when having given the remainder of the house a thorough comb-over, Rob suggested they call it a night and offered her a ride back to campus.

As HIS CAR wound their way through the hills toward the FBI Academy, they discussed what (little) evidence had been found. Rob wanted to know in detail about what the witnesses had said, and needed more information from Jake on what had occurred that evening both before and after the accident.

He told Reilly that he would use his contacts at the police department to obtain copies of everyone's witness testimony. With that information, as well as the police toxicology report, he might be able to form a more complete picture of what had occurred.

"Mayridge, the investigating officer and I go way back. He knows I'll want to take a closer look at this, since Jake is a material witness. Drunken idiot."

Reilly wasn't sure what to say. "He did seem pretty drunk, and a little confused about what actually happened. But I guess they all were, sir." She wasn't entirely sure why she was standing up for Jake, especially since she had no idea if he was involved. "Do the police have any idea who the victim is?" she asked then, changing the subject. "Faye and I didn't recognize him from campus."

"I didn't either, which suggests he isn't one of ours, thank goodness," he muttered, no doubt thinking of the PR nightmare that would rain down on the Academy if the trainee had been one of their own. "I just hope the guy who pushed him isn't either."

"Hope the police find him soon and I'm sorry I couldn't be of more help," Reilly said, frustrated that she hadn't had the presence of mind to look over the crime scene, or check out the partygoers in more detail before the police arrived.

She felt an overwhelming urge to prove herself to Rob Crichton, who had impressed her from the first moment she met him, and whom for some reason Reilly felt was a kindred spirit.

CHAPTER SIXTEEN

The following morning, training got off to a slow start.

It was a sobering pall of grey that hung over the sunny morning and the party attendees' faces. Reilly noticed it at breakfast and so did Faye who unlike the others was chipper and eager to hear what Reilly had learned.

"Not all that much," she admitted. "We examined the crime scene, but we missed talking to any witnesses. Rob'. . . er, SSA Crichton is going to get hold of the witnesses' testimonies from the investigating officers. When Faye's eyes widened, she frowned. "What?"

"Did you just call SSA Crichton by his first name?"

Reilly blanched. "Did I?"

"Yes, you did actually. I don't want to pry, but what is going on between you two? Why did he want you to stay on last night?" She put her hands on her hips disapprovingly. "Is he making passes at you?"

"Of course not," Reilly assured her hastily. "He asked me to stick around because of Jake's involvement — we were first on the scene and he wanted to get some initial observations. And he asked me to call him by his first name last night because saying 'SSA Crichton' all the time when no one else was around got laborious for him, I think. He's an honorable man, I assure you."

"Hmm," Her friend didn't seem convinced. "Well, if he tries anything, you let me know."

"He won't." Reilly was a good judge of character and she knew in her heart of hearts that Rob Crichton was nothing like that. He wouldn't dream of making passes at a student, and she guessed he would be scandalized by the very thought. She knew he was simply anxious about his nephew's involvement in the incident and likely wanted to ensure that Jake didn't end up talking the fall for anything.

LATER THAT AFTERNOON, Rob called Reilly aside after lectures. "I have copies of last night's witness statements from Mayridge," he said. "I'd like it if you and Ms Williamson could run an eye over them, make sure the majority tallies with what you know."

Faye was delighted about the possibility of helping Agent Crichton investigate an actual case. "It's an unbeliev-able opportunity for one-on-one instruction isn't it?"

"He's not officially investigating remember?" Reilly reminded her as they made their way towards Rob's office in the behavioral unit, but she knew what her friend meant. It was an amazing opportunity to have some hands-on involvement with a real live case, and she was going to grab it with both hands and help Agent Crichton and the authorities any way she could.

SSA Crichton's secretary ushered them into his office.

His office was much like he was, Reilly observed — simple, yet classic, but not at all pretentious, functional and comfortable, but not off-putting or sloppy. His desk was good-sized and neat, save for a nearby work-table where Rob indicated they'd be working. Bookcases crammed with reference and crime books, papers, binders filled with notes from past cases; and mountains of files lined the edges of the room, shrinking the square footage considerably and leaving just enough room for the trio to pull out their chairs enough to sit down.

The table itself was half-covered with files, notes, crime journals, psychological studies, and a copy of the new DSM-V, already resplendent with tab markings jutting out of previously referenced pages.

Rob leafed through all the reports and relayed the basics: the victim was a stranger to most of the attendees the night before and no ID had been present on the body during examination. "Any guests who had introduced themselves said he gave his name as Bill," he told them. "And said he came with 'a friend'. Those who encountered him described him as either shy or arrogant. But by all accounts, it seems that the now-deceased Bill didn't converse much. And while he was present in the dining room during most of the drinking game, apparently he only watched, nursing a beer and occasionally cheering a good shot. The majority of witnesses indicated that the victim had left the room and returned a few times prior to the accident, as had all but the most serious of 'contestants.'"

Since most of the witness reports reflected identical stories, Faye and Reilly were able to scan through the accounts more quickly after the first few. Overall, the police had taken a total of 37 reports. Since two of those were from Reilly and Faye themselves, it meant 35 individuals had been present at the house when the accident occurred.

Yet nobody seemed to know the victim.

CHAPTER SEVENTEEN

"The majority seem to agree," Rob said. "Most of the partygoers were in the dining area drinking. It seems the game started with about a dozen guys and a few women, but there were about half a dozen more people watching at the start. Nobody can agree 100% on who started the game, but it seems that Jake was definitely one of the ringleaders. Once the game got rolling and people started cheering and placing bets, most came in, a few more joined, and everybody was pretty plastered by the time the fall happened. Nobody remembered much about the victim, but a lot of these guys don't remember much, period, except that somebody kept bringing in more bottles of water every time they got low."

"What about the person who was throwing up in the downstairs bathroom?" Reilly asked, recalling Jake's story from the night before.

"Right here," said Faye, holding up a statement. "Her

name is Jennifer Hinton. She's a friend of one of the non-academy folks. She came with someone named . . ." here she paused and consulted the report, "Hailey Morris. It says here she's a friend of the guy who arranged the party."

"Yes, I've got the party host right here," Rob chimed in. "His name is Jackson Halvorsen III."

"With a name like that, you think he'd have more class than to let people trash his relative's house." Faye muttered, remembering the ruined lawn.

"So let's summarize what we know so far," Rob went on. "According to the statements, a group of guys — some say three guys, others say about five, including Jake - decide to start a drinking game. The game gets rowdy, the entire party winds up in the room, the booze never ends, and even though people wander in and out, everyone seems to be there except for poor Jennifer, who is unwell. Then Jake who went in search of another bathroom and our victim Bill, who no one seems to know much about and no one really remembers. And of course the person who according to Jake was in a fight with Bill and may or may not have pushed him off the balcony, but makes himself scarce thereafter in any case. Suddenly all hell breaks loose, Jake yells emergency, everyone comes running, and panic ensues."

"What is the victim's full name?" asked Faye. "You said he had no ID on him."

"The police haven't formally identified him yet. We're assuming he didn't drive there, since he told witnesses he came with a friend," said Rob, "so he may not have had his wallet. But it seems awfully convenient that he winds ups dead, and doesn't have a wallet on him. Most men I know myself included, feel like something's missing if we try to leave the house without our billfolds whether we're driving or not."

"I didn't want to be the one to say so, but I thought that was odd too," agreed Reilly, adding almost to herself, "My dad is a drunk who could forget his own kids, but he never forgot his wallet."

Missing Rob and Faye's interested glances, she continued, "I have a few other issues with the whole story. First – like Agent Crichton and I agreed last night, it's odd that such a big, strapping guy like our victim died from a simple fall off a second level balcony at a residential home. Nobody seems to remember this Bill interacting in a volatile manner with anyone, or in fact, interacting at all. Seems most of the witnesses agree that he seemed quiet and even-keel the entire night. Yet Jake says the same guy was involved in a heated argument with someone who is yet unnamed."

"And by all accounts, my nephew had his butt firmly planted in a chair at the head of the table, most of the time leading the whole game. According to most, he had a death grip on a bottle of vodka, which he drank from when he lost. Unfortunately for the police, and indeed himself, he's the only one who was aware of the argument and can tie the unidentified party guest and the victim together."

"But now that we know for sure that the victim didn't get smashed with the others, I'm even more suspicious of his fall," Reilly ventured. "And if he wasn't drunk, which we can assume he was not, why would he lose his temper, especially when he seemed to be interacting with so few people in the first place?"

After an awkward moment of silence, Rob spoke up. "There's something else that bothers me about this whole story," he said. "And it's why I'd hoped you two might be able to shed more light on what really happened at the party."

Reilly and Faye looked at him, wondering what he was going to say.

"It's the whole thing about Jake hanging on to a vodka bottle and drinking from it all night."

At the mention of a vodka bottle Reilly's ears pricked up.

"He's not usually into hard alcohol?" Faye ventured.

"Oh no," Rob replied, "He's quite into the hard stuff. But he usually drinks tequila." He paused, then continued, "One time when Jake was 12 he was staying over at my house – I got called out on a job and he and some friends busted into my liquor cabinet. They got completely drunk on high-proof vodka — a nearly full gallon bottle of cheap stuff left over from a party. Jake and two of his friends downed the whole thing in about half an hour. Threw up everywhere." The older man's expression turned serious. "Jake has despised vodka ever since. He can't even smell it without feeling nauseated. I doubt very much that he was drinking vodka last night." Rob looked at the two women. "And if he lied about that, what else has he lied about?"

The trio sat in silence around the table for a moment. Then Rob continued, "I tried to talk to him again this morning. Of course he was pissed off at me for losing my temper with him last night, and wouldn't say much beyond insisting that he didn't get a good look at the two guys in the bedroom.I asked him to tell me again what had happened. He repeated the same story as last night — almost word for word."

Reilly looked at him. "You suspect it's rehearsed," she stated.

He nodded. "I do."

Faye looked from Reilly to Rob. "Why? What do you mean?"

"Normal memory has built-in glitches," Reilly explained. "Our brains don't have automatic backup, like a CPU. Every time we bring forth a memory and examine it, we change it slightly even if we don't mean to. We then have to re-remember the entire scenario all over again — except now it's slightly different. And that happens every time a memory resurfaces or we tell someone about it."

Nodding in agreement, Rob continued. "Unless it's what's called a 'Flashbulb Memory,'" which is usually attached to a traumatic event, or a complete memorization of something unchanging, we tend to shift things around when we recall, then re-remember them. It's one reason why memories we bring forth from long ago change and fade with time, and why you may suddenly remember something from long ago so clearly if it's the first time you've thought of it in ages," he added.

Faye was contemplative. "So basically what you're saying is, if a person's testimony of an event doesn't shift or change even a little each time they relate it, then it's likely their testimony is memorized? And not a recitation of actual events."

"Exactly." Rob nodded.

"But why would Jake do that?" Faye asked. "He's got to know he's going to get caught if he's lying. He's an Academy trainee for crying out loud."

"Maybe not for long," Rob muttered exasperated. "In order for this to make sense, I perhaps I need to give you a little background. Jake is my sister's son, and was a problem kid since his parents divorced when he was ten. Pretty much all of it was stupid, like getting drunk and fighting. He didn't really mess with drugs I guess because he saw the trouble they cause, and he knew he would never have a career in law enforcement if he started messing around with that stuff. But the one thing that always interested in him was my job, and he had a fascination with the FBI."

"Wait a second," Faye interrupted again, "you mean to tell me that being in the Bureau is Jake's lifelong dream? Then why on earth would he jeopardize it by withholding information about a serious incident, especially when he's so close to graduating?" She looked at Rob. "So he has somewhat of a track record for making poor choices, but doesn't this strike you as odd? Why would he even risk it?"

"Then we have the issue of the vodka," Reilly mused, her heart racing as she understood the implications.

"Exactly." Crichton smiled approvingly at her. "Nice catch Ms Steel. That sharp nose of yours is seriously proving useful."

Faye was confused. "What nose? What vodka?"

Reilly quickly explained her findings from the night before, and how she'd zeroed in on the fact that one vodka bottle in particular had seemed awry. She was right to be suspicious; the alcohol had been watered down or indeed emptied and refilled with water, evidently by Jake. But why pretend to be drinking vodka, never mind make a witness statement in a serious police investigation admitting as much when he obviously hated the stuff? Clearly he had something to hide.

Crichton's tone was muted as he confirmed her suspicions. "For whatever reason, my nephew seems to be covering something up. And I'm worried it's going to mean the end of his career."

CHAPTER EIGHTEEN

L ater that day, Rob headed straight to Jake's apartment.

His nephew had insisted on getting his own place off-campus, despite Rob's offer of free room and board.

"Free room and board from you isn't free," was Jake's response and thinking about it now, Rob realized he had probably been right. Still it seemed his intentions in keeping an eye on Jake from the outset might have been the best idea.

Arriving at the apartment building and finding his nephew's car parked in its usual spot, Rob parked in a visitor slot out of the line of sight of Jake's unit.

He climbed the stairs to the second-floor apartment. Jake used to have a roommate, a guy he knew from college, but Brian had since quit the Academy and moved out a few months before. He knocked on the door and waited for a response.

Given last night's confrontation, Rob thought he might have to coerce Jake into letting him in, so he was extremely surprised when his nephew opened the door. Shutting and locking it behind him, he gripped his uncle in a hug and said, "Am I glad to see you."

Puzzled and concerned, Rob pulled back. "What's wrong? Are you okay?"

Jake laughed mirthlessly and shook his head. "Did anyone see you come here? Did you notice any police patrols around?"

"No, of course not. What are you talking about? You're making me nervous. What's going on?"

Jake led Rob into the living room. Both of them sat on the couch, and Jake leaned close, his voice low as he said, "Remember last night when I told you that I saw the guys fighting but didn't recognize them then went downstairs, and heard a thud?"

"Yes."

"Well, that's not exactly what happened ...."

Rob looked at him. "I didn't think so."

Jake paled. "What tipped you off?"

"The vodka bottle, for one thing. In the witness statement, you said that you took it with you to the bathroom, but you didn't mention bringing it back downstairs. Yet we found it in the dining room. That and the fact that it didn't contain vodka."

Jake looked terrified. "We? Who else knows about this? Mayridge?"

"Relax. One of the new trainees, Steel. I asked her to

look over some of the evidence last night since she was first on the scene . . ."

"Oh yeah, I know her. Bit prim and proper if you ask me..."

"Obviously talented too because she figured out your vodka lie from the get-go," Rob interjected and Jake looked chastened. "Let's get back to what you said before," he continued. "What was all that business last night — especially you pretending to be drunk in front of everyone and when the police were taking your statement?"

Jake swallowed hard and cleared his throat, "You said the vodka bottle in the evidence gave me away. Do you think anyone else noticed I wasn't really drunk?"

"Jake you're worrying me. Tell me what's going on."

"OK – the reason I forgot about the bottle is because I was too busy faking being drunk, and how I only half-noticed the guys fighting." He sighed. "But actually, I did see something."

Rob was horrified. "Then why the hell didn't you tell the police?"

Jake's tone grew serious. "Because here's the thing – I think the police may be involved."

Rob sat back on the couch, mystified. After a long moment he finally asked, "Who?"

"I don't know. Last night, I didn't actually get a close look at any of the cops' faces to compare. But as I was passing by the two guys fighting, I noticed that one of them — not the guy who fell — was wearing shoes that looked awfully familiar — standard issue police shoes.

Then I heard a radio on one of them. It was turned down really low, but I know what a cop radio sounds like."

Rob nodded in agreement; Jake had been San Diego PD prior to acceptance in the Academy so would easily recognize both the shoes and the radio.

"I guess I was just so focused on getting out of there without being seen or heard, I forgot about the bottle when I gave the report. And after I realized a cop might be involved, I was pretty freaked out."

"Yes, but why pretend to be drunk in front of Mayridge and co?" This part was still puzzling Rob.

"How was I supposed to know if one of them had been the guy upstairs?"

"But you'd have known if a cop was at the party surely? Everyone would have."

"Not if he'd been there out of uniform, then changed his clothes or maybe took off his jacket when the police officially arrived."

Rob's mind was reeling. "Are you absolutely sure about this Jake? If one of Mayridge's people are involved..."

"We don't know that yet. Like I said, I don't know much at all, other than something about that setup last night wasn't right. Please Rob, don't do anything until I get a chance to work this out for myself. If that guy, cop or not finds out that I wasn't really drunk and might know what he looks like..."

"Well, what did he look like? You said in your witness report, tall dark-haired and dark clothed with a craggy face ..." Rob knew most of the local force very well, and this didn't ring any bells for any of the guys he was familiar with.

Still, given Jake's suspicions about police involvement and his worries about his non-drunkenness being exposed, he was now even more worried for his nephew.

Jake shrugged. "That part I wasn't lying about. But it was dark and the room was full of shadows. All I can tell you is the guy didn't seem like a student. He was definitely older."

"OK. Come stay at my house until all this blows over. I promise you, I won't hassle you."

Jake looked at him. "But won't it look suspicious if I just all of a sudden go stay at your place?"

"Just say you can't afford your apartment any more since Brian left."

"But my buddies know that's not true."

"So tell them you're trying to save money."

Jake barked a laugh. "They'll *know* that's not true, for sure. It doesn't sound like me."

Rob had to smile, despite himself. "OK. Tell them it's me. Tell them I'm ragging on you to stop spending your dough when you can live for free while you wait for your assignment after graduation."

Jake almost did a double-take. "You actually believe I'll graduate?" he said with dry humor.

Rob clapped him on the shoulder. "Of course you'll graduate. It's in the family. Now get some stuff together. We're going to my place."

CHAPTER NINETEEN

While Jake gathered his belongings, Rob called Reilly and asked her to refrain from mentioning the vodka bottle discrepancy to anyone for the moment, or the fact that Jake wasn't as drunk as he'd appeared.

She agreed, but he could tell she was puzzled and he resolved to explain all when he could. So far she'd proven sharp as a tack, and he wanted her on Jake's side.

Jake reappeared with a suitcase, and they left together in Rob's car. That way, anyone driving by the apartment would assume he was home. Since Jake seemed especially fearful of his safety, Rob insisted on mounting a tiny spy camera at the entrance to Jake's apartment and another inside, just in case any unexpected 'visitors' stopped by. They would monitor the feed on a laptop from his house.

On the ride over, he filled his nephew in on Faye's and Reilly's involvement and the reasons for it, including Reil-

ly's keen sense of smell and incisive analysis of the vodka
bottle.

"Grade-A student, huh. So that's what tipped you off
that I wasn't really drunk?"

"It certainly made me even more suspicious of your
forgetting the detail about taking the bottle to the john
with you. Seems like the smelling thing is pretty unique to
Steel though - I doubt anyone else will catch it." Though it
would be interesting to see if local forensics did catch it —
if not, it suggested Reilly Steel would be one valuable addition for any crime scene investigative team.

AT HOME, Rob phoned Reilly from his land-line and
asked her if she and Faye wouldn't mind coming over to
his house for a discussion. The only reason Jake agreed to
keep the girls involved was the realization that the others
were already aware of his lie, not to mention the fact
that he and Rob needed a trustworthy neutral third party
to keep them grounded, and perhaps pick up any information they might miss by being so close to the
situation.

They couldn't trust the police or anyone else until they
found out more.

Booting up the PC, Rob showed Jake how to scan the
camera file for activity in the vicinity of his apartment as
well as the live feed. Jake scanned the brief time frame
they'd been on the road, but found nothing, so he switched
to the feed. Since there was little movement along the
passageway in front of his place, he knew he could watch

the feed out of the corner of his eye while talking with his uncle and the others.

It didn't take long for Reilly and Faye to arrive at the house.

Jake noticed that Reilly in particular looked very surprised and once again not best pleased to see him. Still she greeted him politely and the three seated themselves at the island in the kitchen. Rob had arranged for some meats, cheeses, crackers and other snacks and they all opted for caffeinated sodas.

Once they were settled, Jake retold all that had happened at the party. "I did see the suspect's face, but I didn't recognize him as anyone I'd seen before. I've thought about it a lot since last night, and I don't recall seeing him at the party beforehand either, so I'm thinking he showed up later and snuck in somehow without anyone noticing." He looked at his uncle. "Then, like I told Rob, I wondered if he just blended in with the police afterwards. And I know he got a good look at me, but I don't know if he knows my name or that I'm an academy recruit — yet anyway." He paused a moment, then continued, "So basically, I spent as much time at the drinking game as possible because I was keeping an eye on this girl I like. It was about an hour and a half after the party started, and I needed a bathroom break, so I went to the downstairs bathroom, but it was occupied, so I went upstairs. There was a long hallway to my right leading to several doors, and a short hallway on my left leading to the master bedroom. I figured a house like this had an on-suite bath in the master, so I decided to go there because it was closer. I went into the bathroom, did my thing and washed my hands, and when I came out, there were these two guys in the bedroom. I guess they didn't realize I was in there. I looked at them as I came out, and they looked at me like I was interrupting something. I had a bad feeling about the whole thing, so I decided to act like I was drunk so maybe they'd think I wouldn't remember them."

Faye nodded. 'Well, you sure had me fooled last night." Somewhat sheepishly, she added, "I thought you were a buffoon."

Jake laughed mirthlessly. "Good. I'm hoping everyone did, because a buffoon makes a terrible witness." After a brief pause, he continued, "After I pretended to stumble out of the bedroom and down the stairs, I paused by the bottom of the stairwell to listen. The drinking game was rowdy at this point, so I couldn't make out any words, but I could hear the men's voices upstairs. They sounded strained and angry, like they were having an argument but trying to keep it down. Their voices got louder, and then I heard grunting, like they were fighting. I heard a couple things get knocked over, then a few thuds in the room, some more struggling and grunting, then a really loud thud that sounded like it came from the back of the house. I rushed out to the patio and found our victim on the ground, not moving. I didn't want to touch anything, and I was worried about the doer maybe still being nearby, so I started hollering for help. Everyone flooded out the door and started freaking out. That's when Reilly and Faye showed up."

"Can you describe the other guy — let's call him the

unsub for the moment?" Reilly asked. "I know a description was in your police report, but I'd rather hear it directly from you. It might ring a bell with us amongst the partygoers we saw."

Jake nodded. Closing his eyes so he could "see" the scene in his mind, he began, "I was across the room from the guy so I'm just guessing, but he seemed to be tall, about 6' or 6'1" probably. The lights weren't particularly bright in the room, but I could tell he had dark hair and heavy brows. His face was kind of craggy-looking, like he had bad acne scars, been in lots of fights, or both. Prominent nose, harsh-looking mouth, thin lips. Obviously, he didn't smile so I can't comment on his teeth. And I couldn't see his eyes well enough to tell you what color they were. He seemed to be the one most concerned with my presence. Now that I think about it, I remember Bill, the victim, looked nervous. But my focus was on the other guy because he seemed angry and so out of place at that party."

"How so?" Faye enquired.

"Because he wasn't a student and he wasn't dressed for a party. He was wearing dark clothes and heavy-duty shoes with thick waffle soles. I smiled at him like I was a drunken idiot, said something like, 'Hi, great party huh?' and laughed. The guy glared at me, and I stumbled out of the room and down the stairs." Jake opened his eyes and said, "That's it."

The group sat in silence for a moment; then Rob spoke up. "Well, I think the first thing we need to do is check out the crime scene again. Last night, I didn't get to go over it as thoroughly as I'd have liked. Jake, it's important for you to continue to support the belief that you don't remember what the guy looked like, so you can't be seen to be curious about the crime at all."

"No problem there," said Jake, stealing a glance at the laptop monitor, "I just want to lay low until they catch the doer. That guy looked like a roadmap of bad decisions and harsh circumstances. I don't want anything to do with him."

"I'd love to have another shot at the crime scene," Reilly piped up earnestly. "Something Jake said about the shoes. Heavy-duty soles with deep ridges, right?"

"Yeah, kind of like military or police issue," he confirmed.

"Okay. Faye, remember the lawn?"

Faye thought a moment, then opened her mouth in a silent "O". "You're thinking whoever it was might have picked something up on his shoes if he snuck in across the lawn."

"And I'm also betting he left something behind," she said, thinking of Locard's Exchange Principle and how the perpetrator of a crime will always bring something into the crime scene and leave with something from it. Turning to Rob, she continued. "Has the homeowner returned yet?"

"I'll check with Mayridge."

Rob duly placed a call to the investigating officer, and discovered that no one had been able to reach the home-owner Barbara Smith, who was on a long sojourn via private boat. The police chief had left a message for Ms Smith about the incident at her house at the next sched-uled port of call, which was about three days hence. Apparently, she had just departed her last stop the night of the party.

"Okay, we're set," said Rob as he hung up the phone. "The chief gave me permission to go back in as long as I make sure everything is left the way I found it. But I was only able to convince him to allow one other person to come with me to assist, and I really had to sell him on it, which wasn't easy."

"Mind if I go?" Reilly raised an inquisitive eyebrow at Jake, asking for his permission.

"No problem. Like I said I want to lay low, and I don't think the cops would appreciate my nosing around anyway."

Faye looked a little chagrined to be left out, but took it in her stride. Knowing she was too keyed up and full of questions to go back to her dorm room and study, she pulled out her cell phone and called fellow classmate and computer geek Jordan Nance. She wanted to research Jackson Halvorsen III, the organizer of the party and also the homeowner of record, and she needed Jordan's expertise.

"OK then Reilly," Rob announced, heading for the door. "Let's do another sweep of the crime scene - see what we find this time."

He didn't have to ask her twice.

CHAPTER TWENTY

When Rob and Reilly returned to the house, it was deserted. Rob retrieved the house key from a nearby lockbox, and using the code the police chief had given him, broke the seal on the front door.

Ushering Reilly into the house he closed and locked the door behind him. Then pulling several latex gloves from his jacket pocket, he offered her a pair. Snapping them on, they moved on into the dining room.

Reilly had brought a proper camera this time, and used it now to snap several photos of the dining area, table, bottles and cans, and once again the vodka bottle Jake had watered down.

She also took some wide-angle shots of the room, as well as close-ups of stains on the chairs and carpet from spilled beverages. Investigating the spills and sniffing them, she concluded that most of the stains came from beer. Spills from hard alcohol seemed to be confined to the table. The room was beginning to smell unpleasantly stale, and that sickly cologne was now making her stomach roil.

Moving into the kitchen, they took stock of the kitchen supplies, primarily refrigerator and cupboard contents. Other than a few bags of chips and some dip, which it appeared the partygoers had brought themselves, no food seemed to have been consumed. Cabinets containing alcohol had clearly been raided, and two empty cardboard cases from a domestic canned beer, one in the fridge and one crushed in the garbage, bore testament to the prolific alcohol consumption of the attendees. Reilly was once again glad she and Faye had missed all the "action."

"I want to take a closer look at that upstairs balcony," Rob said when they'd finished with the kitchen, "then work our way down the stairs and out to the patio. Follow Jake's footsteps, see what he saw."

Reilly followed him upstairs and into the master suite. Again, it bore all the hallmarks of a scuffle. A reading lamp had toppled from a small table, the chair beside it was overturned and the draperies hung askew, as though they'd been pulled, perhaps to prevent a fall.

He and Reilly began to move around the room, looking for anything pertinent or relevant, although they weren't sure what they should be looking for. Other than a few objects overturned, the room seemed normal. Reilly snapped pictures of the room as a whole and took close-up shots of all the disturbed and overturned items.

"I want to look for trace from the Man in Black's

shoes," she said, referring to Jake's description of the unsub. "I take it you brought some evidence bags?"

Rob smiled. "Remember that officially we're only here to observe," he chided her. Then, dropping his gaze, he indicated his right jacket pocket from which he pulled out a small stack of about half a dozen evidence bags.

She grinned at him, but only said, in what she hoped sounded like a disappointed tone, "Of course. I'll just look." Getting on her knees near the sliding door, she began to search the carpet. In the meantime, Rob went into the en-suite master bathroom.

Reilly moved along the edge of the sliding door's track, using a flashlight to illuminate the area so she could see more clearly. She didn't have far to go; there were a few clumps of mostly dried mud on the carpet near the sliding door track.

She took several photos of the dried mud. The CSI team had already combed the area, so Reilly had no compunction about picking up a small piece. She carefully placed it in the evidence bag and marked it exactly as Rob himself had taught her.

Looking further, she noted that a bit of the dried mud had also fallen into the sliding door track, and there was a blade of grass there as well. She again took photos but did not disturb the evidence.

MEANWHILE, Rob had gone into the master bath to look for clues. The toilet seat was down which made sense to him. Jake, for all his bad habits was perpetually neat, and one of his pet peeves was an open toilet seat. According to his testimony, Jake should have been the last person to use this toilet, so a closed seat rang true to Rob.

He looked on the floor, around the toilet and near the bathtub, but it seemed clean. Rob took photos of the floor and toilet using his own camera, checked and bagged trace with a cotton bud, then opened the medicine cabinet.

You could tell a lot about a person from what was in their bathroom medicine chest. In all Rob's years of crime scene work, he'd had several occasions where simply the contents of a medicine cabinet provided useful evidence.

Looking through it, he discovered a variety of items one would typically expect to see in a bathroom cabinet: bandages; antibiotic ointment; calamine lotion; a bottle of rubbing alcohol; and a dark brown bottle containing hydrogen peroxide. He also found a toothbrush holder containing one toothbrush, a nearly full prescription in the homeowner Barbara Smith's name for a benzodiazepine, and a bottle of men's cologne with a brand name he didn't recognize.

Returning to the bedroom area, Rob told Reilly what he'd found and she showed him the dried mud on the carpet and the bits of mud and grass in the track. He was pleased she had left the evidence in the track alone, as he wanted to make sure the CSI team hadn't missed it.

Then he mentioned the bottle of medication. "Odd that someone on an extended trip would leave their medication behind?" she commented.

"Especially an anxiety/sleep medication." Rob agreed.

"But maybe she doesn't need it anymore. The date is eight months old."

Moving back into the bedroom, Rob said, "Before we check out the balcony, I need to confirm something." Locating the bedroom's walk-in closet, he opened the door, turned on the light, and stepped inside.

Reilly could tell he was rummaging around and taking pictures. He then emerged from the closet. "There are no men's clothes hanging in there and what few things there are is limited to socks, underwear, a couple T-shirts, and a pair of jeans in one drawer. Also some cologne in the closet. But I don't see any men's shoes either."

"So the guy who threw the party doesn't live here," she concluded. "Ms Smith lives alone but has someone staying over now and again?"

"That's what I was thinking. Come on; let's take another look at the balcony."

The duo walked over to the sliding door, and stepped out onto the patio balcony from where the victim had fallen to his death.

CHAPTER TWENTY-ONE

It was dark now, but Rob quickly located a porch light, which illuminated the area well. He began to walk around the balcony area, inspecting the disarranged patio furniture and paving, while Reilly concentrated on the balcony railing.

They worked in silence for several minutes, checking for trace, snapping photos and looking things over.

It seemed quite natural to Reilly to work this way, and she found she was very comfortable working side-by-side with another investigator collecting evidence. Being somewhat of a loner, she always felt her weakest area was working with others, so she was glad she felt relaxed instead of tense, as she'd expected.

Finally, she called Rob over to the balcony railing. It was wooden with intricate carving along the handrail. Pointing to a small section, she said, "This area is damaged, so it's a good bet our victim went over here." The rail, which was of considerable thickness and well-made, was cracked in one spot as though someone had slammed against it. "I took photos from several angles," she said. "There's no trace that I can see — the wood didn't splinter as you'd expect. It cracked, but it held."

"And what would you deduce from that?" Rob asked. Ever the tutor, he wanted to see if she'd draw the same conclusions he had.

"It suggests that the victim hit the railing hard," she replied, "hard enough to crack a wooden railing that was made to withstand cracking." She paused and then continued, "Which leads me to believe the fight intensified quickly, and the victim was shoved very hard from a fair distance." She thought for a few moments, wrinkling her nose and staring at the railing. Finally she said, "I'm not sure this was accidental after all. Looks like the victim was slammed against the railing and shoved over on purpose."

"I wonder if the police came to the same conclusion," Rob said, nodding. "I looked over the paving out here and I checked the furniture," he told her. "However, I think we should do a more thorough inspection of the ground near the damaged railing, see if we can find relevant trace to support the theory."

They both got down on their hands and knees, inspecting the area, but found nothing of immediate interest. Rising to their feet, Rob looked down to the pool area below.

"I'm still wondering how the doer got into the house. It's possible he snuck in the front door, but I'm betting not since he picked up some debris from the lawn. It seems to me he came in from the back through the sliding door, which again fits Jake's theory that he wasn't one of the partygoers. I want to figure out how he got up here."

TROOPING downstairs and to the back of the house, Rob found the porch light and turned it on. This light also proved to be more than adequate for their purposes, but they still kept their flashlights at the ready for inspecting dark corners.

Again, they moved and worked in silence, looking over various areas of the yard.

Reilly went toward the gate on the side of the house that separated the back yard from the front, while Rob gravitated toward the far end, where a tool and potting shed stood. Turning on his flashlight, he inspected the area around the shed. Quite quickly, he found a small folding ladder tucked in the shadows nearby. Suspecting the man in black might have used it to obtain access to the house, he carefully inspected the steps. No clumps of dried earth were present and there were no specific footprint patterns, but the steps themselves were dirty. The dirt could easily be from several seasons of gardening, Rob thought, yet he didn't want to risk damaging potential evidence, and he wasn't sure if the CSI team had noticed the ladder. Still, he needed to test his theory.

Just then Reilly returned.

"The gate was unlocked," she reported, "and there were some footprints with a waffle pattern in the mud near it on the front yard side. I took measurements and photos of the tread and a sample of the mud."

"Good job," Rob told her. "Now maybe you can help me with a little theory I have." Taking the ladder to the area below the balcony, he opened it up and said, "I found this tucked in a dark little cubbyhole near the shed. I figure the location of this ladder is either awfully convenient by chance, or awfully convenient on purpose, and I'm not one to believe in chance."

Reilly picked up on his thought. "You think this ladder was left here for someone's pre-planned use?"

"Indeed," Rob confirmed, "I'm 6' tall, about the height of the unsub if Jake's description is correct. I'd like to see if I can grasp that railing and pull myself up from a ladder this height, but I don't want to damage any evidence by stepping on it. It doesn't look like it was processed. I'm betting no one knew it was here."

Reilly looked around for the picnic table. Spotting it, she took the ladder over to it to compare height. The table was about two inches shorter than the top step of the ladder, but Rob figured it was close enough to be worth trying, so the pair moved the picnic table in place under the balcony. Standing on it, he was still able to grasp the bars of the railing and pull himself up and over the balcony, so he and Reilly concluded the ladder had probably been used, potentially as an access point by the unsub. Rob made a mental note to ask the chief if it had been processed by forensics. But why had the guy come in that way and not through the front door? Jake was right about that much; obviously he wasn't supposed to be there.

Coming back over the railing and climbing down, Rob looked around the yard.

"You know, it really isn't that far from here to there," he commented. "This whole thing is really weird."

His gaze landed on the back of the house and rested there a moment. He was about to look away, but something nagged at him.

It seemed there was an awful lot of exterior wall for the size of the bedroom. It was a large master suite, but the wall seemed disproportionally large out here.

Reilly caught his frown. "What's bothering you?" she asked.

He glanced at her, then looked back at the wall. "Take a look at this wall," he said. "Does anything strike you about it?"

She stood there, trying to figure out what he was seeing. At first, nothing came to her, but then she spotted it. "That wall is pretty long on the one side of the balcony," she said, "but I don't remember the room being that long."

"That's what I thought too," Rob replied. "I want to go back inside and look at that room again. But let's use the stairs this time," he added wryly.

CHAPTER TWENTY-TWO

U pstairs in the master bedroom, Rob and Reilly stood near the end of the bed and looked around the room once more, keeping in mind the outer dimensions of the rear of the house.

"It seems quite a bit smaller than it should now I'm inside again and comparing it with the outside dimensions," Reilly said.

Scanning the room with fresh eyes, she noted that all seemed in order until her gaze fell on the far side of the room.

Rob seemed to see it at the same time. Their eyes met and by unspoken agreement, they moved to the wall on the opposite side of the king-sized bed.

Everything seemed ordinary — a bookcase of average depth flanked by wall sconces, with a comfortable-looking chair and ottoman under the sconce nearest the sliding door. The small table had apparently been knocked over in the fight, and there were several old book volumes on the floor; perhaps pulled from the bookcase during the fight?

"I know this might seem ridiculous, but I think there's another section of room behind this bookcase," Rob said.

"I was actually thinking the same thing, but I thought it sounded too 'haunted house' to mention." Shooting Rob a mischievous smile, Reilly said, "I can't help myself, I have to do this." She began trying the most cliché attempts at finding a hidden door — pulling on the light fixtures, tugging on various books to see if they operated some kind of lever.

Rob soon joined in the search and they went through the entire bookcase in this manner, but nothing happened.

"That would have been too coincidental and too easy if that had worked," Reilly mumbled frustrated, "but it was worth a try. I have another idea though." She began to run her fingers along the outer edges of the bookcase, and he began doing the same on the opposite side. Unfortunately, they found nothing. Figuring they were either wrong about a hidden room or unable to find the controls because they were well-disguised or located elsewhere, they prepared to complete their search. It was getting late, and both had early morning classes to look forward to.

Rob wanted to take a look at the upstairs wing opposite the master suite, so they turned on the hall lights and moved down the hall, opening doors and looking in rooms. Other than the bathroom, which had obviously been used by party guests the night before, no other rooms seem to have been disturbed.

After ensuring that all was in order, they left the house.

Rob made sure it was locked, then replaced the key in the lock box.

REILLY WAS WELL and truly exhausted by the time she arrived at her dorm room.

Faye was still awake, dying for details, and her enthusiasm gave Reilly a brief second wind, so she uploaded the images from the crime scene on her computer, and she and Faye looked through them together. When Reilly got to the shots of the bookcase, which she and Rob had both photographed extensively, Faye became very excited.

"A secret room?" she exclaimed. "That's like something out of an old horror movie. But from what you said, it sounds plausible. I wonder where the controls could be."

"They've got to be portables somehow," Reilly replied. "Remote control, maybe. Or very well hidden in any case. We did look in the nightstands and dresser drawers, but I don't recall anything that could be a remote for a secret room. Of course, we weren't considering such a thing when we searched those areas. I should go over the photos of again, see if I can spot anything that might contain a remote." She paused, yawned conspicuously and said, "But not tonight. It's way past my bedtime. I need some shut-eye."

But she couldn't deny that she again felt disappointed and frustrated that she and Rob had made no eureka discoveries at their second sweep of the house.

Still as Rob told them often enough, this was par for

the course with crime scene investigation and she'd better get used to it. Gather pieces of the puzzle little by little until a bigger picture is revealed.

Unfortunately patience had never been Reilly's forte.

CHAPTER TWENTY-THREE

Rob arrived home to find Jake still awake and watching the camera feed on the laptop.

"Anything happen while I was gone?" he asked.

"Actually, yes," his nephew replied, looking edgy.

Rob sat down beside him, and Jake continued, "Right after you left, I scanned the feed during the time we were talking to the girls to make sure I hadn't missed anything. About 45 minutes ago, I saw this." Accessing the program, Jake brought up the data from earlier. He scanned backwards until a dark figure appeared in the frame, then went back a bit more until the figure vanished from shot, then let the video run forward.

Rob watched as the dark figure moved into screen view, heading for Jake's apartment. He must have been aware of the camera or at least suspected it, because he kept his face downcast so his features weren't visible. He was tall, probably 6' or so and his hair was dark. He was dressed all in black, and wore a pair of black leather gloves.

Rob stared as the figure rapped hard on Jake's door, then without waiting for a response, tried the doorknob. Finding it locked, the man looked into the peephole, which unintentionally revealed part of his face.

"Think that's our man in black from the party?" he queried, disconcerted.

Jake nodded. "I'm almost positive. But watch what he does next."

The figure onscreen again tried the doorknob, then rapped on the door. He waited about 15 seconds, then apparently satisfied Jake wasn't home, took out a cell phone, called someone, spoke into the phone briefly, hung up, then moved out of view. "I wonder who he was calling," Jake mused.

"Has anything happened since?"

"Not yet. I can't help but wonder what's going on off-camera, though. It's too bad we don't have eyes in the parking lot."

"You're thinking about your car?"

"Yeah. Seeing that guy make a phone call, then not return to my apartment, makes me suspicious. I expected him to try and access the place, but once he made that phone call and didn't return . . ."

"We'd better check out the car before anyone drives it." Given Jake's suspicions, they couldn't be too careful. "I think I've just about had it for today," Rob continued yawning. "I need to get some sleep. You should too. Morning comes early around here."

THE FOLLOWING MORNING, both awoke refreshed, despite receiving their less-than-usual amount of sleep.

Jake was dragging a bit, suffering from the memory of disturbing dreams involving the man in black. It had finally sunk in — the unsub not only remembered Jake's face, but he also knew who he was and where he lived. But how could he have found out so quickly?

And more to the point, what was he planning to do if Jake had been home?

Coming into the kitchen, Jake found his uncle already awake, preparing a breakfast of English muffins, hard-boiled eggs, and juice. "Coffee's hot and ready," Rob said cheerily by way of greeting. "I forgot how you take it, or I'd have poured you a cup already." Giving Jake a closer look, he grew serious. "You look tired. Are you okay? Didn't you sleep well?"

Jake shook his head. "I guess I'm more worried about this guy than I thought."

"I can imagine, but try not to worry. You're safe here, you'll ride in to the Academy with me. I've already sent Mayridge a copy of the footage from your place last night. They're running it through a facial recognition program to see if they can identify him. We'll keep you safe."

Jake sighed. "I hope you're right. I'm just a little spooked by the fact that the guy found out who I was so quickly."

"I was thinking about that too," Rob replied. "Obviously, somebody tipped him off. That hints at the possibility of one of the partygoers besides the victim, knowing him."

But who was that person? And if his nephew was just an innocent bystander, why did the man in black feel the need to check up on him?

CHAPTER TWENTY-FOUR

During the first class of the day, SSA Rob Crichton announced to the recruits: "Last week, we took a run through Hogan's Alley. Starting this week, we'll be spending a lot more time there.

Reilly couldn't wipe the smile off her face; she was thrilled to be going back to Hogan's Alley.

"The scenario today will be a CQB, or Close Quarter Battle, scenario," Rob continued. "Meet at the entrance to the town at 1:00 pm sharp. We'll be joined by the advanced recruits, who will help coordinate the event."

Reilly could hardly wait until 1:00. She was almost too excited to eat lunch, but she knew she'd need energy to perform effectively. While they ate, Faye filled her in on what she'd been up to the night before.

"I did a bit of digging on the guy hosting the party," she began. "Jackson Halvorsen III is quite the cad, actually. He goes to Old Dominion University. I have a feeling his dad pulled some strings to get him in there. He's barely keeping his place; in fact, he's on academic probation as we speak, so it's likely this little incident will reflect negatively on his scholastic career as well as piquing the police's interest in him. He already has one DUI here in Virginia and another in DC His license has been revoked and he's not supposed to be driving, but he has a car registered in his name in another state, so I'm guessing he's not obeying the law. He lives in a dinky little apartment near the university - I'm guessing because his parents cut his allowance off and will only pay certain things that directly affect him staying in school, and there's a limit. Apparently they're determined, despite all the evidence that supports the conclusion their nephew is a moron and should just live at home with them forever, to force him to get some kind of degree and at least pretend he'll have some useful future career sometime before he's 40." She paused.

Reilly's mouth was open. "How on earth did you find all that out?" she asked, impressed by her friend's sleuthing and the fact that she'd rattled all of that off without taking a breath.

Faye grinned. "Jordan Nance. He's really very smart and amazing with computers. And don't worry," she added breezily, seeing Reilly's look, "everything we got is above-board and available from public sources. Jordan just happened to know which sources to access. And there's more. His father, Jackson Halvorsen II, made a great deal of money in the personal computer industry in software coding; he got in on the ground floor and did a good job of hanging on to the rights, so he's set for life and so is his only nephew, Jack – or Junior as his family calls him. Dad is known as "Big Jack," by the way, and apparently he keeps a low public profile but has a very big ego. He's publically criticized his only child multiple times in print, which is saying something since he's rarely quoted. The kid has a rap sheet, all petty stuff, mostly drug offenses and writing bad checks, beginning when he was 12. Junior was smart enough to keep the dollar amounts of the checks low enough so it wouldn't be grand theft. That was after his dad kicked him out of the house and cut him off the first time, by the way, when Junior was about 18. They reconciled about 2 years ago, when he convinced Big Jack to put him through school. Big Jack agreed, but Junior started blowing it during the first semester. He's on his last legs with his dad. Junior just turned 26 last month, but he behaves more like he's 15.

Reilly sat mesmerized as her friend continued. "Big Jack knows all the "who's who" of the software field, and there's a rumor that he's friendly with some unsavory characters in ... other fields as well. Let's just say they're the kind of businessmen who carry semi-automatic weapons with them to business meetings. Why a man like Big Jack would be involved with organized crime, I don't know; it's all just rumors, but they're abundant. There are quite a few dangerous folks who are rumored to be in Halvorsen II's inner circle, but no proof exists, and no one dares accuse him openly."

"Great," said Reilly sarcastically. "Junior's dad's rich, and has 'friends'. Just what we need. But I thought the house was owned by someone else, so what was he doing hosting the party? And how did we get invited?"

"He's a good friend of Terry Nordingham's and as for the relative ...well I have a theory about that ... As we know, the name on the deed is Barbara Smith. I also did a little digging on Ms Smith, who happens to be a former employee of one of Big Jack's earlier business ventures about 28 years previous. She received some kind of stock option from that company, even though she only worked there for about 18 months. She was his secretary." Faye paused meaningfully on the word, letting Reilly fill in the blanks.

"You think she might actually be Junior's mother?" she said, hazarding a guess.

"Could be — why else would he call her his relative?" Faye replied. Then her tone changed, "But there's something else we didn't know and I think it's a bigger problem."

"What?"

She took a deep breath and went on, "There are reports online about the accident. They mention Jake as a material witness and one of the articles has a photo."

"Damn. We'd better tell Rob and Jake about this," Reilly said, "Especially when Jake's hoping to lay low." Glancing at her watch, she continued, "We've got about ten minutes before we're supposed to be at Hogan's Alley. I say we head over there now and try to talk to them before the exercise starts. Though, on second thoughts, maybe we should wait until afterwards. We don't want to throw Jake off his game."

"Maybe we should just head over there and see if we can find Rob first," Faye suggested. "He'd know what best."

CHAPTER TWENTY-FIVE

When they arrived at the entrance to Hogan's Alley, they were relieved to see Rob already there. Faye discreetly informed him of the news articles mentioning Jake by name. As they expected, he was very concerned and explained what Jake had seen on the camera feed.

"That's got to be how the guy figured out where he lived," Rob said. "Did any of the articles have photos of Jake?"

"One of them did. It looked like an Academy head-shot," Faye told him.

Rob swore. "That's what I was afraid of." He looked up as more recruits filed into the area. "Look, why don't we meet again later — at my house again so as not to arouse any suspicion on campus. We can fill Jake in and talk things over then."

Agreeing, Reilly and Faye took their places with the

others gathering for the training exercise including Jake who waved over, but looked tense.

Rob addressed the group. "As I mentioned this morning, this will be a CQB run. We won't be using many live participants for this, as we're more interested in having you practice the formation and techniques, particularly distinguishing friendlies from hostiles. They aren't color-coded, so you'll have to pay attention to the illustration on the pop-up silhouette itself. Your hostiles will likely be holding a weapon, but make sure what you see is a weapon, and not a baby or loaf of bread, before you shoot.

"We'll be using DM9 dye paintball guns, which are less messy than traditional paintball guns but just as effective for marking hits. We'll be using flash powder for explosives, which is more smoke than substance, but it can still burn you, so be careful.

"I'll now turn the floor over to Jake Callahan, who's going to instruct you on how you'll proceed through this exercise. Jake?"

Addressing the group, Jake said, "The exercise we'll be running is Close Quarter Battle techniques. You may hear this referred to in some circles as CQC, which stands for Close Quarter Combat. Same thing.

"Now, our scenario is to find an unknown number of snipers and other hostiles. Some threats are pop-up silhouettes, some are real people. Some have explosives. You will not know when or where the threats will appear, and remember, not all silhouettes that appear are hostiles. Our goal is to move through the area, cover each other while navigating a tight, hostile environment, neutralize hostiles, and complete the scenario without any loss of friendly or agent life. You will receive commands from the lead agent, which today will be Julia Woodridge, one of our senior recruits. The other team leader today will be Dan Webster." Jake indicated both leaders, then continued, "SSA Greene and I will observe the exercise from the end of the alleyway and indicate when the exercise is over by shouting, 'Game!'" There will be considerable audio distraction to simulate the noise and panic of an actual situation. Are there any questions before we split into groups and the team leaders explain the formation?" Most members of the group shook their heads 'no,' so Jake continued, "Okay, we'll proceed as follows: I'll be splitting everyone into two groups comprised of agents from both classes so the newer recruits can learn from the more experienced recruits. We'll assign the groups in a minute. Once the training exercise begins, your entire focus should be on the event. In your mind and attitude, it must be real. Remember, here's where we practice. If you make a mistake here, it probably won't end your life." His voice was terse. "Out there, it can and often does."

CHAPTER TWENTY-SIX

"You'll be going down an alley between two rows of tightly spaced buildings." Jake informed the recruits, some of whom looked terrified.

"There are both hostiles and friendlies on rooftops, so watch out for that. Your team leader will head the formation, which will run in a straight line along one side of the alley. Your team leader will give commands, but Woodridge is the lead, so her word is final. Depending on your assigned position on the team, you'll be responsible for specific duties during the exercise, but you should be aware of all your surroundings. This is what it means to be an agent, people — you have to have eyes all around your head."

Reilly caught a quick, meaningful glance from Jake before he continued, "We'll be dealing with obstacles as well as live actors. Some will have weapons, some will have explosives, and some will have both. They will try to rattle and distract you and make you break formation. That's their job. Your job is to ignore that and secure the scene. The exercise will begin on my signal right after the auditory distraction begins. Are there any questions?" No one had any, so Jake assigned the groups and the team leaders explained the specifics of the formation to their respective teams. Jake had put Faye and Reilly on separate teams. He tried to make it a habit to "break up" roommates during exercises so recruits would become comfortable working with those they might not know well.

After the teams had been briefed, they lined up in formation at the end of the alley, one team on each side. "Okay, everybody clear the exercise area! Recruits, get ready," shouted Jake and the recruits, weapons in hand, poised themselves for action.

From numerous unseen stereo speakers, a heavy-metal rock song from the early 2000s issued forth at high volume. It happened to be one of Reilly's favorites, which proved additionally distracting because her mind instantly focused on the song. Pulling herself away from the music, she focused on her team leader.

Jake made eye contact with Rob, then with Julia. Giving her a nod, the exercise officially began.

With a hand motion from Julia to Dan, the two groups moved forward, single file, against the buildings on either side of the alley. Julia's group took the left side; after scanning the area, she motioned Dan to take his team into the first building on his side of the alleyway. Single file, Dan in the lead, his team entered the first structure while Julia's team held their position and one team member from the other team remained in the alley to cover the rooftops on Julia's side.

From one of the rooftops opposite Reilly's position, the first silhouette appeared. She spotted it and fired, hitting her target after about 4 blasts. Silhouettes continued to appear sporadically as her team covered the alleyway. Dan's team returned from the first building and covered the alleyway while Julia's team entered the first building on their side. Reilly had been chosen to stay outside and cover the alleyway.

In the middle of the alley, a flash went off near a bicycle, as though the 'explosive' had been thrown from a doorway. Some recruits flinched, but no one broke formation. Continuing as planned, Dan's team waited for Julia's team to reappear before they entered their second doorway, where the 'explosive' likely came from.

Entering their second building, Dan's team found and secured a live suspect. One recruit kept control of the prisoner, maintaining the next-to-last position in line. In a flowing, coordinated manner, the teams crept forward, taking turns entering and securing buildings, watching for silhouettes, and anticipating flash blasts. The recruits were confronted by several more hostile pop-up silhouettes and a couple of friendlies, as well as another live suspect with a "detonator" for his flash. As the teams neared the end of the alleyway, all seemed secure, and Reilly noticed a few recruits letting their guard down in anticipation of the end of the exercise. Her instructors had prepared for this, however, for just as the last of the recruits exited the building and made their way around a barrier at the end of the alley, another flash went off. You could tell who had let their guard down; those people jumped.

"Okay, that's game. GAME!" shouted Jake, and the recruits began to relax, although many kept looking around, still startled by the final flash blast.

"Game, everybody. Are we clear?" Jake shouted, and received confirmation from the team leaders.

The music ceased, and the recruits met Rob and Jake in the middle of the alley.

"That looked pretty good," he said to the group. He paused briefly, then added, "You also managed to hit every silhouette." Reilly could tell many in the group thought this was a compliment. Jake could tell also, because he said, "That's not a good thing. There were a couple friendlies in there. Does anyone know who shot the friendlies?" Jake knew because he'd made a mental note of it; he wanted to see if the students could figure it out. Unfortunately, they didn't. Jake was met with silence and averted eyes. "That's a problem," he said. "Know your target, people. We'll have to work on that. And it was clear many of you let your guard down toward the end. That final blast was a test to see who was still 'all in the game'. Some of you weren't — and that can be deadly in the real world, so keep that in mind. Otherwise, it looked really good, especially for a first run."

"Yes good job, everyone," said Rob. "That'll do it for today. You have a little time before your next class, so if you want to take a look at the recording of alley exercise or the alley itself, you're welcome to do so, although you'll be doing a full critique of the footage in your tactical analysis class tomorrow. Jake will go pull up the footage, so if you're interested, follow him. I'll stay here to answer any questions about the exercise or the alley itself." Rob caught Reilly's eye and she subtly indicated she wanted to stay in the alley. He indicated his agreement and she quickly began to look around the scene of the exercise.

Moving through debris and trash, she made her way to site of the first flash powder blast. Inspecting the area, she noted the flash pattern on the cement, then moved into the building from where the 'bomb' came. She looked around the room, then exited, moving towards the site of the second blast.

Reilly kicked at the debris where the subject had been standing when he 'detonated' the blast. The live subject had been holding a dummy detonator, Reilly remembered. She investigated the area, but found nothing of importance on the ground. As she began to inspect the rusty truck the subject had used for a shield, Rob, who had been moving around the area speaking to various students, arrived at her side.

"Ms. Steel," he greeted her and she returned the greeting with a brief nod. "That was a great exercise. I know it only lasted a few minutes, but it was very intense. So what are you looking for?"

"I remember the suspect detonated the second flash using what I assume was a dummy detonator?"

Rob shook his head. "No, that charge actually was a little more than just flash — we used an actual detonator for that one. Something the guys in the lab are perfecting — making a wireless detonator that's compact, sturdy, and conceal . . ." His voice trailed off as he noticed Reilly's wide-eyed expression. "What is it?" he uttered quietly.

"Help me find that detonator," she replied, hunting with renewed fervor through the debris at her feet. Looking around for nearby students then leaning closer to Rob, she whispered, "The hidden room controls in the house. I bet . . ." Now her voice trailed off as she focused fully on her search.

Leaving Rob to the ground, she stood and tried to replay the scene of the second explosion in her mind — the suspect had squatted behind the front end of the rusty pickup, then rose to his feet and detonated the blast. The mechanism in his hand was box-like. She remembered seeing the suspect hit with a dye mark, and he went down. Moving to the front of the pickup, she began to search the area. After a few minutes, she found the control box inside the rusty front. The suspect must have dropped it at the perfect angle for it to fall into the crevice of the large, double-bar metal bumper. Retrieving the box, she called Rob over.

"As I suspected," she said certain that she'd hit on something relevant to their visit to the house the night before, "it's a hinged box with the control panel inside. And it opens kind of like a *book*."

CHAPTER TWENTY-SEVEN

At the end of the day, Reilly and Faye went directly to Rob's house. This time, Jake greeted them at the door.

"He went out to pick up some food," he informed them. "Should be back any time now. Do you want something to drink?"

Both women opted for sodas, but this time, Reilly asked for one with no caffeine.

Jake chuckled at that. "So you've already been a victim of the 'FBI Recruit Insidious Caffeine Increase'?" he joked. "We all go through it. You'll find that lots of caffeine is an occupational hazard, though you're smart to avoid it when you can. Otherwise, you can get kind of immune to it. Rob used to work with this one agent who drank so much coffee when he worked for a PD that by the time he got to the Bureau, drinking coffee made him fall asleep."

The three of them chatted about trivial things while

they waited for Rob. He arrived shortly and the group settled down to a meal of chicken, side dishes, and dinner rolls. Everyone was hungry, so they ate mostly in silence, punctuated by compliments about the chicken, mashed potatoes and gravy.

After they'd finished eating and cleaning up all four retired to Rob's living room.

"I found out the victim's cause of death," Rob informed them. "He probably could have gotten up and walked away from the fall except for one thing — he was a hemophiliac."

Reilly nodded, thinking that his sudden death from such a short fall now made sense. "Not only did the disorder make him bleed excessively when injured, he was also in danger of developing brain aneurisms if he fell. The coroner found one in his brain from a previous fall, probably sustained while playing sports in high school or college. Apparently, when he hit the ground Saturday night, the aneurism burst and the victim died almost instantly, which is why there wasn't much blood from the head wound."

"Wow," said Faye. "So it really was kind of a freak accident. Poor guy."

Rob brought his laptop over and showed them the footage from Jake's apartment the night before. They all agreed that the individual at the door fit his description of the unsub at the party.

Faye then explained to Jake about the articles and photo of him online.

"Damn it," he spat, "So much for lying low."

"I found out some other interesting information," Faye continued, relaying what she'd learned about the Halvorsens and their connection to Barbara Smith.

"What do you mean, she could be his birth mother?" Jake queried, puzzled.

Faye filled in the blanks. "Well, Big Jack married his wife about 8 months before Junior was born," she said. "There's no searchable records on this, I'm guessing because Big Jack is good at covering his tracks, but too many other things add up for it not to be the case. Barbara Smith was Big Jack's administrative assistant; she was hired right after Jack started the company with money he borrowed from his soon-to-be father-in-law, a wealthy rancher named William Parker Hobson. Big Jack's fiancé, Sarah Hobson, had convinced her father a mere 6 months before to lend Big Jack the capital for his enterprise. Everything was going fine; then suddenly, Barbara was laid off with a generous package that included some stock options. About a year later, Big Jack sold the company, and the handful of stockholders which included Barbara made a fortune. Shortly thereafter, she bought the house. But for several months prior to the sale of her stock, she virtually disappeared.

"About six months before the company sold, Sarah and Big Jack, who'd married shortly before Barbara was laid off, decided to adopt a child. That child was Junior." Faye paused, then continued, "I just can't see any other reason for a secretary, even a really good one, to score a stock option layoff package after only a year and a half of employment, especially when it was already obvious that such a package would be worth a lot of money when the company sold. There was also three month's pay included, but that wouldn't have supported Barbara for an entire year, and there are no records of her working for several months following the layoff. And the timing for the adoption is suspicious too — about nine months after Big Jack and Sarah were married? I can't help but think that someone was paying Barbara's expenses for a while so she could stay home — and no one would realize she was pregnant, nor would anyone find out she'd given birth."

"So you think Big Jack had an affair with Barbara, got her pregnant, and paid her off to disappear for a while then let him and his new wife adopt the baby once it was born," Jake concluded.

"It seems like the only logical conclusion."

"Okham's Razor," Reilly said, glancing at Rob who preached the philosophy on a daily basis. "If you remove the impossible, whatever remains however improbable, must be the truth. So if Junior is Barbara's son," she pondered, "was he part of the argument at the party? Did it have something to do with Barbara?"

Jake shook his head. "From what I can remember, it didn't seem that way. I didn't hear much of the details but it sounded more like a personal beef between two guys. I don't know..."

"OK so let's recap what we do know," Rob suggested, taking out a notepad and pen. "First of all, we know that the guy who pushed our victim was tall, dark-haired with a craggy face and heavy brows, wearing dark clothes and heavy boots. Anything else come back to you about him, Jake?"

He shook his head. "I've thought it over and over again, and again I'm almost certain he wasn't at the party before I saw him in the master bedroom upstairs."

"Suggesting, like we thought," Reilly commenting, "that he didn't come through the front door, but used a small ladder to access the balcony. I am guessing the sliding door had to be unlocked, because there's no evidence to the contrary. That indicates a prior arrangement, if you ask me."

Everyone nodded in agreement, and Rob continued, "As far as Bill the victim is concerned, all witness statements agree that he drank, talked, interacted little and seemed to come from nowhere. No one mentioned knowing him previously. Then suddenly, he's upstairs in the master bedroom with this craggy-faced stranger, and after a brief but intense argument, he winds up dead and the other guy is nowhere to be found." He paused a moment, then added, "I think our best course of action at this point would be to find out more about Bill, and research any connection to the homeowner. Faye, did you come across any mention of a "Bill" or "William" associated with Junior?"

She thought for a moment, then replied, "Not off the top of my head, but then again I wasn't really looking for that. I can scan through my information again though. I saved it, and I have the USB drive with me. It's in the car." She grabbed her keys.

"My camera's in there, too," Reilly said. "In the glovebox. Can you get it for me? I'd like to take another look at the pictures I took at the crime scene."

"Be right back."

Rob went to call Mayridge and find out if the police had learned any more about the victim and his background. While he did so, Jake asked Reilly, "So how are you finding training so far?"

"I'm loving every minute," she replied enthusiastically. "I'm learning so much, though I'm a little short on sleep." She chuckled, "And there was this asshole VirtSim instructor the first week . . ."

He shook his head, smiling. "Are you ever going to let me live that down?"

"Probably not."

"Actually, now that I think of it, I want to pick your brains about something," he said, in a confiding tone.

Reilly looked at him. "Oh, what's that?"

"Do you think Faye might let me take her out sometime? She's great."

And maybe Jake Callahan wasn't such a jerk after all.

CHAPTER TWENTY-EIGHT

"I just talked to the chief," Rob said, coming back into the room. "They've now formally identified the victim. His name is William Thompson."

"Great, at least now we have a starting place," said Reilly.

"How about we divide and conquer?" Rob suggested. "Faye, since you're our resident super computer sleuth, will you do the honors and chase up some info on our victim William Thompson? You can use my laptop."

"No problem."

Reilly spoke up. "I'm going to go over the photos of the bookcase at crime scene and see if I can figure out which book might be hiding the controls to that secret room. I'm certain there's one there. It might not have anything to do with the crime, but if I can figure it out, at least we can tell the police and they can investigate it."

Rob nodded, and said, "In the meantime, I'll run

through the trace samples and see if anything strikes me. Jake, would you mind scanning the feeds from your place again? I went by earlier during a break in my day and set up a camera on your car. I know it's kind of after the fact, but maybe we'll catch something anyway." Jake agreed, and the group settled in to work.

AN HOUR PASSED before anyone paused in their work or spoke.

Then Rob looked up. "Why don't we take a little break? I know I could use one."

After they'd reassembled, Reilly began updating the others on what she'd been doing.

"I had a hunch on campus earlier about the control box for the secret room. When Rob and I were at the crime scene, we couldn't find any control or mechanism that allowed access, so we figured it was very well hidden — possibly remote, or both. Then today, after the exercise at Hogan's Alley, I was poking around the scene and something Rob said about a remote used for one of the flash blasts struck me. Once we found the remote device from the exercise, I was certain — one of the books must be a fake. Inside are the controls to the room. So I decided to look over my shots from the bookcase area in the master bedroom. When we explored the crime scene, I noticed several books on the floor and assumed they'd been pulled out of the bookcase during the fight. After all, the table was knocked over." She passed around the relevant photos for the others to see and get a sense of the crime scene. "I ruled out books being stacked on the table prior to the fight, mostly because the table was small and there were several books, so it didn't seem logical they'd fallen from there. Looking again, I still believe that's true; however, I think the doer knew about the secret room controls, and pulled some books out of the bookcase while looking for the correct one."

"You think he was in there alone and maybe Bill interrupted him?" Jake mused.

"That's what I'm guessing."

Faye looked thoughtful. "Not to get uh ... overly personal, Jake, but how long do you think you were in the bathroom?"

Jake thought for a moment. "Well, I always wash my hands after I use the restroom, so probably two, three minutes tops."

"Do you remember if the sliding patio door was open when you entered the room?" Reilly asked.

He thought about it again. "I don't think so. I wasn't looking that direction, but I don't recall feeling any wind or hearing any 'outdoor' noises if you know what I mean. So I'm pretty confident it was closed."

"If you didn't hear anything outside, either the man in black wasn't there yet, or he was lying in wait," Reilly mused. "He could have been just outside the door on the balcony, or in the room crouched down out of sight for all we know."

"Yikes," Faye said, shuddering. "Our unsub in the room, watching and waiting for Jake to leave . . . What if Bill hadn't come in? He could have gone for Jake instead."

Jake looked fondly at her. "Don't worry, I can take care of myself."

Looking embarrassed now, Faye cleared her throat. "Well, I was able to find out who Bill is — or was, I guess," she said. "At first I couldn't find much on William Thompson — I don't have a social security number or property records and since his is a fairly common name, identifying the correct William Thompson that way wasn't going to work. Since no police reports mentioned him, I decided to cross-reference the name with Barbara Smith's records." Her eyes shone with enthusiasm and Reilly realized that her friend was born for this kind of work.

"It took a bit of digging, but I found Will Thompson, a former boyfriend I guess, who lived with Barbara for about ten years after the whole Jack/Junior affair. I am assuming that it was shortly after she purchased this house, because ten years ago, Will Thompson used to work for a company that specialized in safety and security equipment. Guess what their specialty was?" She paused for dramatic effect and smiled. "Panic rooms."

"What's a panic room?" Jake asked, looking blank.

"What — you never saw the movie?" Faye teased.

"It's a dedicated room for use in case of an attack or intrusion," Reilly told him. "They're state-of-the-art, usually contain a cot, some provisions, emergency first aid supplies, and a dedicated emergency line. And most importantly from our point of view, they're accessed by a hidden control that once activated, can only be opened from the inside.

"Exactly," Faye agreed. "And one of the most popular customised features is a safe."

"Is that's what the man in black was looking for – the safe?" Jake pondered. "So are we talking an interrupted robbery then? What was he trying to steal?"

Faye continued. "While looking into Barbara's history, I happened upon some recent financial information. The house has two mortgages and with current property values, she's upside-down. She also takes a lot of trips most of which over the last couple of years have managed to travel through or wind up in Las Vegas. I smell a gambling problem ...."

Rob nodded. "Good work all round guys, lots to think about. Mayridge knows I'm taking a look at everything in addition to his team, and I've promised to update him on any findings. I'll give him a call now." He checked his watch. "But it's late and you guys have another busy day ahead. Go home, catch a few hours and we'll put our heads together again tomorrow, maybe head down to the station and talk to Mayridge directly."

Reilly was disappointed. She planned to stay up all night, sifting through evidence, imagining possibilities and hopefully finding answers.

For her, the closer they were getting to a breakthrough, the more addictive the hunt was becoming.

CHAPTER TWENTY-NINE

The following day on campus, although rigorous, dragged on for Reilly.

She was anxious and nervous about visiting the police station. The information they'd gathered was valuable, and meetings with police chiefs and investigative teams everywhere would be commonplace for her once she became a full-fledged agent, so she figured she might as well get used to it. One thing was for sure, she guessed it would be a million miles from her last visit to a police station, where she'd needed to formally identify her mother's body...

WHEN TRAINING WAS OVER, Faye and Reilly took a quick jaunt to their dorm to freshen up then headed over to Rob's house, who informed them the chief would see them in about an hour's time.

They set out in Faye's car, Rob at the wheel. A buddy of his in college had owned a Mustang '65 — and he had enjoyed driving that car whenever he'd had the chance, and jumped at Faye's offer to let him take the wheel. She rode shotgun, while Reilly and Jake sat in the back.

The police chief, who knew Rob well greeted them cordially, then ushered them in to his office where Mayridge awaited. "As you can probably tell SSA Greene is a big fan of 'on-the-job experience,'" the investigating officer joked to the recruits. "But we're grateful for any angles you guys have to offer on this case." Reilly guessed that like most police departments, the investigative team were over-worked and understaffed.

The chief confirmed as much. "We certainly could use all the help we can get," he continued. "We're short-handed and this case is growing cold real fast. We got nothing from a fingerprint scene and the crime lab's backed up for weeks. And we can't interview the homeowner because her boat hasn't reached port yet."

"I think we can help you there," Rob told him. In turn, the group explained all they'd discovered: the "drive by" at Jake's apartment, information about Barbara Smith, her finances, and her connections to the Halvorsen men as well as the victim, Will Thompson, finishing up with their suspicions about a panic room in the master bedroom.

When they'd finished, the chief and Mayridge thanked them and promised to inform Rob when they'd had a chance to follow up on the leads they'd provided.

As they left the chief's office, Rob saw another officer

he knew and stopped to chat. The squad room was busy, so Reilly occupied herself with watching the goings-on of the officers. As she stood there observing, a couple of uniforms walked past behind her and she caught of brief whiff of cologne...

CHAPTER THIRTY

All of sudden, she was transported back to the first time she'd run through the scene at the party house, where she was almost certain she'd come across the very same musky and potent scent, from someone at the party she'd thought. She couldn't identify or catalogue it, but she trusted her instincts, especially her sense of smell.

Turning around, she scanned the area. She saw a few officers who could have been wearing the cologne, so she waited for Rob to finish his conversation.

"Do you know any of those men?" she asked indicating the officers who'd just walked past her.

"Just one of them," he replied, pointing out the heavier-set man in discussion with a tall, somewhat lanky officer. "Let me ask the chief about the other guy," he told Reilly, and went to find him.

"He's new," the chief confirmed. "Came highly recommended but so far, all I've seen is a lot of ego. I made him

sergeant, and suddenly he thinks he's bucking for my job."
The chief frowned. "He might not be with the department
long," he confided. "I've just about had it with his sloppy
work. He never seems to be where he's supposed to be."

"What's his name?" Rob asked.

"Ted. Ted Travers. But the guys call him Teddy Terrific
because he's always bragging about himself."

"Would he have been one of the first responders at the
Smith house?" Rob asked, and when the chief looked
curious he added, "Reilly says she recognized his cologne
from the night of the accident."

"He was actually." The chief looked dubiously at Reilly.
"Your sense of smell is that good?" he asked. "Pretty handy
for a crime scene investigator, huh."

ONCE THEY'D RETURNED to the car, Rob filled the others
in about the officer with the distinctive cologne. He also
dropped a bombshell about the bottle of men's cologne in
Barbara's bathroom cabinet.

"I took a sample, so if think you could compare ..." he
said to Reilly, whose heart raced.

"I'd know it anywhere," she commented. "And I
thought it was interesting that the chief mentioned he was
new. If as Jake says, he thinks a cop might have been
involved ..."

Could this Ted Travers be their mysterious man in
black? What Jake had said about him perhaps changing his
clothes and blending in with the police afterwards, it made
sense.

Faye looked up. "I'm happy to do the honors in checking Officer Travers out."

Later, Faye duly sought out Jordan Nance, her fellow recruit and computer geek. After promising him she'd fill him in fully once everything was over and done with, he agreed to help her research Officer Ted Travers. They spent hours working and by the end of the day, had found some interesting information. Faye was almost bursting, but she kept the discoveries to herself, vowing to wait until the others were once again assembled at Rob's house before relaying the information.

CHAPTER THIRTY-ONE

"It turns out our new officer on the force, the obnoxious Ted Travers, is one slick dude," Faye told them. "He's worked for about half a dozen departments in as many years; he always manages to get himself involved in something or suspected of something, but squeaks out of it somehow and moves on to another department in another city. Before this, he was a prison guard at a maximum-security prison in California. He was terminated for smuggling contraband to prisoners. None of us got a good look at him yesterday but ..." she pulled a printed headshot photo of Officer Travers from her handbag and showed it to the others.

They gasped, almost in unison.

The face in the photo was craggy, dark-haired, and heavy-browed. It looked a hell of a lot like Jake's description of the man in black.

"An ex-prison guard?" Jake exclaimed. "Well I guess that explains why the fight got nasty so quickly."

"OK, before we jump the gun on this, why don't we go through the facts as we have them so far, see if we can figure out what Travers and Bill were fighting about," Rob suggested.

"First who knows who," Jake began. "Our main players are Junior Halvorsen, William Thompson Barbara Smith and Officer Ted Travers, right?"

"That's our crew," confirmed Faye. "Seems Junior is most likely Barbara's illegitimate, disowned child. Given Officer Ted keeps a bottle of his famous cologne in Barbara's bathroom cabinet, we can assume he's Barbara's current squeeze and victim Will/Bill is potentially an ex. Does that about cover it?"

Reilly said, "Sounds more like a soap opera when you put it that way."

"Now that's an interesting angle," Rob said. "Let's use that for a minute — what could a soap opera view of this crime tell us about the motive?"

"Ooh I think I see where you're going with this," Faye said. "In a soap opera, with all these connections, my first thought would be a jealous love triangle?"

"Maybe, but in that case, wouldn't Bill have been going after Travers? He must have known that Ted or even Barbara wouldn't be there, because otherwise I doubt he would have attended otherwise," Reilly observed. "Unless . . ." she paused a moment. "Do you suppose he saw the party going on, decided to stick around and protect Barbara's place from her blockhead son Junior?"

"And in the process, managed to interrupt a robbery?" Reilly suggested, thinking again about the safe in the panic room. Bill must have known about that.

"That's a good theory," Rob agreed. "One thing bothers me, though. I still think the robbery if that's what it was, was planned rather than coincidental. Based on Jake's remembrance of events, the men weren't arguing when he came out of the bathroom — they waited until he'd left, like they knew each other or something. If you came upstairs in a friend's house and found a stranger breaking in, would you stop to chat with him first, or would you restrain him and yell for help?"

"That's true," said Jake. "Chances are you're going to clobber the guy first and ask questions later. So that makes me think maybe Bill and Travers know each other."

"Or know *of* each other," Reilly put in. "Maybe Bill found out about the robbery somehow, and came there specifically to thwart it?"

"Another good theory," Rob agreed. "Let's think about this a minute. Okay, Ted is dating Barbara. I'm thinking perhaps he knew Barbara had something of value and arranged to steal it. Bill found out and came to the party to intercept him."

"It's a theory," agreed Faye. Looking at Reilly, she said, "Uh-oh, you've got that look on your face. What's up?"

"What look?" Reilly asked.

"That look where you wrinkle your nose and kind of purse your lips a bit," Jake said. Faye laughed and said, "Yup, he's got it. That's the look."

Reilly blushed furiously, not noticing Rob looking on, trying not to grin.

After a brief pause, she cleared her throat and said, "I was thinking about Barbara's finances. If she's underwater, don't you think she'd have sold off everything of value by now? What would be there to steal? Then I thought, insurance scam."

Jake was nodding. "Makes sense. But here's something that's been bugging me — why didn't Junior recognize Travers at the party? If he was involved with his mom, wouldn't they have met?"

"Maybe he didn't see him," Faye suggested. "Especially as it seems Travers snuck in afterwards so Junior wouldn't have seen him."

"If we assume that's true, then my guess is Junior had nothing to do with any robbery the night of the party." Reilly said. "The chief said he seemed clean. But here's something else — apparently Barbara's ship left its last port the night of the party."

"That seems rather convenient. Add to that the fact that she's scuba diving in her living room, and you have a reason for a robbery," Faye finished.

"Exactly," said Jake, taking up the story. "So Barbara must have something of value in that panic room, and she figures if it's stolen, she can collect the insurance. She asks her new boyfriend Ted for advice, and he comes up with the plan."

"Right," said Reilly. "And I just can't think of any other reason for the sliding patio door off the master bedroom to be left unlocked, or the books to have been gone through.

Travers had to have known about the controls in the book, though perhaps he forgot which one it was. When I looked through the photos, I saw several similar-looking volumes that could hide a set of controls."

"So if Ted Travers is the robber," Faye said, stating the obvious, "then he also must be our killer."

CHAPTER THIRTY-TWO

A t the Academy the following morning, Rob asked Reilly, Faye, and Jake to join him in his office during lunch break; he had some important news.

"I've called the chief with the new information last night," he told them, "and he called me first thing with some good news. Ted Travers was arrested on a manslaughter charge at 2:00 this morning. He'll be terminated and most likely prosecuted for his part in the attempted robbery too."

Reilly looked delightedly at Faye. They'd done it; they'd solved their first case.

"Which brings us to the next point — during the official interrogation, Travers confirmed that he was trying to find which book he was supposed to use to open the panic room but Bill interrupted. That's about when Jake came out of the bathroom."

"So we were right," Reilly said, with some satisfaction.

"It turns out that Bill and Barbara are still close, and he had discovered Barbara's faux-robbery plan and tried to talk her out of it. When he found out she planned to go ahead, he figured out the details and made a point to be at the party. When Bill confronted Travers, he told him he was not going to allow him to go through with the plan. Travers tried to bribe him with an offer to cut him in for some of the profits, and Bill was insulted. The argument ensued when Bill told him in no uncertain terms that he was going to call the police. A fight ensued and Travers did shove Bill at the railing but thought he would catch himself before falling over the balcony, or worst case scenario, would walk away with a concussion. He had no idea Bill had hemophilia."

"What about Barbara's son, Junior?" Jake asked. "Was he in on it too?"

"Mayridge called him back in for questioning this morning. Junior knew nothing about the plan; but Barbara had suggested that he take care of the place while she was away and he jumped at the chance to throw a party in a big, fancy house and drink all the booze. Clearly Barbara knew her son well and guessed the party would provide the perfect cover-up for the robbery."

"So what were they trying to steal?" Reilly asked, again wondering what a gambling addict would have of value.

"According to Travers, she had some rare coins in the panic room safe. The market is too weak at to pay her enough by selling them the moment, but years ago the insurance might have been set very high, so the theft of the coins would pay well. And she knew that if she were out on a boating trip, she would be blameless if — when — a theft occurred at her home. And as Reilly suspected, she turned to her new lover – Ted Travers serial conman — for ideas. He agreed to help her."

"And it all backfired when Bill showed up," Faye observed.

"Indeed it did," Rob agreed. "And even though no one aside from us in this room and the police can know the extent of your involvement, ladies, I must say your combined efforts really did blow this case wide open."

Reilly smiled broadly, even though Faye had done most of the investigative work and she doubted she'd done anything at all particularly helpful. Still, she enjoyed basking in Rob's praise.

"Well, Faye did most of the work," she admitted.

"On the contrary, your assessment of the crime scene and finding the panic room, not to mention your sense of smell at the station was the key to identifying Travers. If you hadn't pinpointed the cologne, we never would have made the connection to Barbara and he'd still be at large. And if you hadn't found the panic room, we wouldn't have considered a robbery."

Jake smiled. "So now Ted is off the force, and will stand trial for the crimes. Barbara Smith will probably plead out, but she'll likely lose her home at the very least. Overall, I think justice will be served."

"Good work people." Rob smiled at them all, unaccountably proud of his Quantico recruits.

EPILOGUE

FOUR MONTHS LATER

"May I now introduce our honorary graduate speaker as chosen by her peers, ladies and gentlemen, Reilly Steel."

Blushing heavily, Reilly stood up at Rob's introduction and the crowd applauded as she made her way to the podium.

Even though her hands were shaking, she tried to keep her voice even.

"Fellow recruits, now newly minted FBI agents," she began, smiling proudly at the words, her gaze sweeping over the crowd, "We have come through a lot — twenty weeks of tough training, challenges and growth, both personal and professional."

Her gaze honed in on a familiar face in the crowd, Faye, sitting alongside a handsome figure, Jake Callahan whom her friend had been dating for several weeks now. Faye was smiling at her with such pride, she was practically glowing.

It felt good to finally have such friends.

"And now," Reilly continued, "as we stand ready to face even bigger challenges, we celebrate our achievements — friendships made, bonds forged, and lessons learned.

And as we go forward as agents to protect our country and Her citizens, may we be imbued with strength, wisdom, intelligence and . . ." here she paused a moment, looked over at Rob, and smiled as her instructor gave her a proud nod, "an instinct for the truth."

FROM THE AUTHOR: We hope you enjoyed this short-novel prequel to the CSI Reilly Steel series.

Check out the full length novels in the series available now, or download Books 1 - 3 and save 50%.

Read on for an excerpt of TABOO - book one in the Reilly Steel series.

TABOO - CSI REILLY STEEL #1

Forensic investigator Reilly Steel, Quantico-trained and California-born and bred, imagined Dublin to be a far cry from bustling San Francisco, a sleepy backwater where she can lay past ghosts to rest and start anew.

She's arrived in Ireland to drag the Garda forensics team into the 21st-century plus keep tabs on her Irish-born father who's increasingly seeking solace in the bottle after a past tragedy.

But a brutal serial killer soon puts paid to that. A young man and woman are found dead in a hotel room, the gunshot wounds on their naked bodies suggesting a suicide pact.

But as Reilly and the team dig deeper and more bodies are discovered, they soon realize that a twisted murderer is at work, one who seeks to upset society's norms in the most sickening way imaginable...

PROLOGUE

San Francisco Bay area, California

'Go on, Reilly, I dare you.'

'Jess, forget it – I'm not doing it, OK?' Reilly Steel trundled along the path on her way home from school. Her younger sister skipped along in front of her, her fluffy blond pigtails bouncing with every step.

She hated picking up her sister from school — all her friends got to hang out at the mall, but no, she had to go get Jess, take her home, give her a snack, make sure she did her homework. 'You know Dad says we should stay away from him,' she said.

Twenty yards ahead, an old man walked slowly back and forth across his yard, raking leaves. Dressed in an old flannel shirt and dirty overalls, he had a pronounced stoop, thin silver hair raked across his head and large gnarled hands wrapped round the handle of the rake. It was fall; the leaves were turning on the trees, the sun sinking lower in the sky with each passing day.

Jess looked at Reilly, her clear blue eyes shining with mischief. 'Go on, say something to him.'

'Didn't you hear what I just said? We're not supposed to talk to that guy.'

'But why?'

Reilly exhaled in annoyance. 'Why what, Jess?'

'Why aren't we supposed to talk to Mr Reynolds?'

She glanced at the older man and shivered. Randy Reynolds they called him — word was he had a taste for little girls. Jess was staring at him, her eyes wide with fascination as though she half knew the truth.

'He's a bad guy. He ... does things to little girls,' Reilly said, finally. She gave her sister a nudge. 'Come on, let's get going.'

Jess didn't move. 'What kind of things?'

Reilly sighed. She knew her sister well enough to recognize that look – Jess wasn't going anywhere until her question had been answered. 'Well, he likes to ... touch girls—'

'Touch them?'

'Touch their bits, you know ... like their private parts,' she continued, uncomfortably.

Understanding suddenly dawned in Jess's eyes. 'Eeew! Why would he want to do that?'

How to explain to a wide-eyed ten-year-old when in all honesty Reilly didn't get it herself? 'I don't know,' she mumbled. 'I guess some guys just do.'

Jess looked thoughtful. 'He's not supposed to do that though, is he?'

'No. Like Dad always says, nobody touches your private parts

except you.' She nudged her again. 'Come on, let's go. We've got lots of homework, and you know Dad'll get mad if it's not done before he gets back from work.'

Not only that but Reilly also had to make dinner and clean the house, all the things a mom should do.

But not their mom.

She and Jess started walking again, closer to Reynolds' house. As they passed, the old man stopped raking. He looked up, his eyes glistening as he watched them walk past.

'Hi girls.' His voice was a low croak.

Reilly said nothing and kept her head down, but Jess stared right back, insolent, looking him straight in the eye. 'Jess, I'm warning you,' Reilly muttered out of the side of her mouth.

'You're a pretty one, aren't you?' Reynolds said, his mouth breaking into a grin. Jess stared back, a defiant look in her eyes. Reilly grabbed her hand and tried to haul her along, but she pulled free.

'You like little girls, don't you?' Jess challenged. She stepped forward. 'You want to touch my private parts, right? Go ahead then.' And with that, she lifted her skirt and flashed her pink cotton Snoopy pants at him.

'Jess!' Reilly cried, flabbergasted.

Reynolds stared transfixed – evidently torn somewhere between surprise, lust and shame. Then just as suddenly, Jess dropped her skirt, picked up a stone and hurled it with all her strength. Caught off-guard, the man stumbled backward and landed in a crumpled heap on his lawn.

Jess turned and ran, grabbing Reilly's hand as she raced past. 'Come on!'

They didn't stop running until they were around the corner.

Breathless, Reilly looked at her little sister. 'What the hell were you doing, Jess? You don't flash at people ... Don't you ever do something like that again!'

Jess was wide-eyed. 'Why not?'

'Well ... because it's just not the thing to do.' Reilly struggled for words. 'We were told to stay away from him. You could get yourself in serious trouble.' She shook her head, amazed but also faintly impressed at her brazenness. 'I can't believe you did that.'

Jess looked back at her with innocent eyes. 'You said he's a bad guy. And bad guys are supposed to be punished, aren't they?'

1

Dublin, Ireland

Reilly's head shot up off the pillow and she stared around her, momentarily forgetting where the hell she was.

She took slow, deep breaths in an attempt to calm her heart rate, and let her eyes gradually adjust to the shadow-filled room.

Lying back down, she stared up at the ceiling, the lights of the passing cars creating abstract patterns as they slid by in the rain-slicked streets below. Her thoughts wandered in a random, half-asleep manner and wound up back with Jess.

It had been a while since she'd dreamt about her sister. Maybe a year or more, which was good; Dr Kyle, her shrink back home, would have been proud of her. The less she dreamt about Jess and the less she thought about Jess, the better.

Because thinking about her, about *it* had never got Reilly anywhere. Although Dr Kyle would probably argue that thinking about Jess had had a profound influence on Reilly in every conceivable way. In fact, the doc had implied more than once that if the whole Jess situation had never happened, then she might well have decided to follow a very different path. But he was a shrink so of course he *would* say that.

Her thoughts had brought her full circle, wide awake in a dingy Dublin apartment in the middle of the night. Sleep was gone for now so pulling back the covers, Reilly got out of bed and headed for the bathroom.

She switched on the light and gasped at the sight in the mirror. A bright red scar ran along one cheek and she rubbed furiously at it, hoping the seam mark from the pillow would go away. Her eyes were glassy and swollen from lack of sleep and her fair hair was tousled, knotted and badly in need of a trim. A quick wash and shampoo would just have to do for now she sighed, stepping into the shower.

A few minutes later, she wrapped herself in a towel and padded barefoot into the kitchen. Or at least that's what the cheery real estate guy who'd rented her the place had called it – as she far as Reilly was concerned, it was nothing but a glorified broom closet. But apparently in this town, a broom closet for a kitchen was all you got for the best part of a thousand bucks a month, and for that, Reilly had also been blessed with a 'modern open-plan living area' and a 'cosy bedroom'.

If you considered coffins cosy, she'd wanted to reply. But at least the place was in better shape than anything else she'd seen, and at the time she'd needed to find somewhere to live – fast. By then the hotel bills had started to mount up, and her employers were bitching about the expense.

Dublin had come as a shock to her – no strike that – *Ireland* had come as a shock to her. Growing up back home in California, her father used to love telling her and Jess colorful stories about the country of his birth; it sounded almost magical – a land full of green open spaces and welcoming, friendly people. She never tired of hearing tales about Mike Steel's childhood before the family's eventual emigration to California.

But upon her arrival four months before, Reilly quickly realized that the slow-paced, easy-going picture of Ireland her dad had painted didn't fit at all with the Dublin she found.

Instead of the laid back and carefree natives he'd described, Reilly was faced with a population of supremely confident, well-educated and ambitious go-getters, even though like the rest of the world, Ireland had recently suffered its fair share of financial turmoil and unemployment.

While Reilly was under no illusion that working in Dublin would be a holiday, she was already taken aback at level of serious crime in the country, particularly one with such a small population.

She fixed herself a coffee and turned her attentions to the day ahead. Although it was already 7.30 a.m., it was so dark outside it still felt like the middle of the night. It was days like this she really missed the sun coming up over San Francisco Bay – that she missed the sun, period.

She closed her eyes and pictured the view from the

headland back home where she usually parked her car – the wide sweep of the bay, the breakers rolling in from left to right, the sea that deep, dark green that she loved, white-caps calling to her as she hauled on her wetsuit and unloaded her surfboard from the top of her car.

By contrast, winter here was oppressively bleak and miserable – at first, Reilly couldn't understand how people even managed to rouse themselves from their beds, let alone summon the energy to work as hard as they did through those dark, gray days. But despite being starved of sun, Ireland was now Reilly's home and, sixteen weeks in, she was just about beginning to get used to it.

Not that she'd had the opportunity to spend all that much time outside, though. Since moving to Dublin, she'd been practically chained to the lab, which she supposed was a good thing. Labs tended to be the same all over the world and the one place in which Reilly felt most at home.

'Or the one place you feel most in control?' Dr Kyle had suggested, and maybe he was right. In the lab, surrounded by familiar equipment and implements that always did her bidding, she felt at peace.

Albeit temporarily.

Reilly shivered and, pouring the last of her coffee down the sink, she returned to her coffin-cum-bedroom and began to get ready for work.

The spartan office was lit by two lines of fluorescent lights, which cast a harsh light on the long table. Reilly spread a collection of evidence bags across the table and watched as her team wandered in, coffee cups and notepads in hand. They jostled each other, raced for the prime seats like kids in school, then finally settled and looked up expectantly at her.

'OK, what have we got?' she asked, glancing at the array of bagged and labelled items on the table in front of her. There was a bloodied T-shirt, a broken beer glass, a half-eaten burger and some fries – or rather, 'chips' as they were listed on the inventory.

One of the lab assistants, Gary, cleared his throat and peered at the report. He was the most confident of the bunch, in his late twenties with shaggy brown hair and small wire-framed glasses. 'According to the report, it's from an assault in Temple Bar.'

A popular tourist area of the city Reilly knew, full of restaurants and pubs.

'Yeah, it can get a bit rowdy down there at the weekends.' Lucy said quietly. Lucy was the only other girl in the group, a honey-pot the guys constantly buzzed around. 'Big groups of people out of it, not to mention all those hens and stags.'

'Hens and stags?'

Lucy flicked her blond hair back from her face and Reilly immediately caught a scent of her perfume. One of those celebrity-endorsed ones she figured, trying to place it; *Lovely* or *Amazing* – something like that? 'You know – last night of freedom before getting hitched?'

'Ah, bachelor parties, you mean.'

'Yeah. They usually get pretty wild.'

'Pity it's gone like that. It used to be such a nice area, all cobbled streets and old buildings.' They all looked at Julius. He was the only one older than Reilly, a career lab tech with the social life to prove it. She hadn't memorized all the details of his personnel file, but she did remember that he was forty-two, unmarried, and had worked at the forensic lab for over fifteen years. *Now there was an unusual profile for a lab tech*, she thought, sardonically.

These gatherings gave her a good feel for the team; their individual personalities, who excelled in certain areas and who didn't. Because this job wasn't just about collecting evidence and analyzing it to death, it was about spotting the small things, the tiny, seemingly insignificant threads that could suddenly bring an entire investigation together.

It was that great feeling, the immense thrill of chasing – and eventually finding – that crucial piece of evidence which had kept Reilly going all throughout her studies at Quantico, and later during her time with the California Police Department.

Her determinedly hands-on approach was one of the reasons the Irish Police Commissioner had offered her the job of 'dragging the technical bureau into the twenty-first century' in the first place. And if Reilly was going to get the brand new Garda Forensic Unit operating like a well-oiled machine – as per her brief – she knew she needed to keep its employees stimulated and interested in the evidence, rather than have them locked away carrying out mindless analysis in the recently built, state-of-the-art crime lab.

Hence this morning's gathering.

'There were some witnesses,' Gary went on, 'but apparently it all happened very fast ... most of them were trashed, so they can't tell for sure who clocked him. The cops'll need a solid description before they can charge anyone.'

Reilly wasn't personally familiar with Temple Bar and made a mental note to go down there and take a look around. Since taking the job, she had spent much of whatever free time she did get walking through different parts of the city getting to know the surroundings and could now easily differentiate between the cobblestones at Dublin Castle to those situated around Trinity College – knowledge crucial to their work.

'Anyway,' Lucy grabbed the report from Gary, and continued reading, 'according to the cops, there was a bit of aggro, two men got into it, it quickly got nasty, and now one of them is unconscious in Bishop's Street Hospital after being glassed with a beer mug. The bloke who attacked him legged it before the police got there.'

Reilly nodded, translating Lucy's slang as best she could. 'OK, what else? CCTV?'

'Hold on ...' Lucy quickly scanned through the report. 'Nope. They've got some, but they can't make the bloke out. Footage is blurred and there were too many other people around.'

'OK,' Reilly turned to the others. 'Anyone got any thoughts?'

'Well, we can test the blood on the T-shirt,' Gary ventured.

'Which tells us what exactly?'

'It'll tell us whose blood it is for one.'

'But we know whose blood it is,' Julius pointed out. 'Obviously it belongs to the guy who was injured.'

'Yeah, but it was a two-way fight, remember?' Rory, as usual, had bided his time before speaking. 'Maybe the attacker bled too, which means there might be two different samples on there. If there is, we can get a comparison sample from the victim, eliminate him, and then we're left with the sample from the guy who did it.' Rory was a rugby player, with a big build and dark, intense eyes. With his huge hands and crooked nose, he looked as though he himself knew a thing or two about street fights.

'That still won't help us identify the attacker, though, will it?' Lucy said, turning to Reilly who had remained silent, content to let the team figure it out amongst themselves.

'OK, so it won't help us identify him *now*,' Rory conceded, 'but it will give us something for later, won't it?'

'Good point,' she agreed. 'But is there anything else here that could help us identify him, something we could use to give the police some kind of a definite description of him right now?'

There was a brief pause as the team contemplated this.

'Fingerprints from the pint glass,' Gary suggested, eventually. 'Although, I suppose that's only good for a comparison too, isn't it?'

'How about the burger?' Lucy's tone was studied. 'It says here that the attacker was eating a burger just before the fight, so we could analyze his saliva for DNA.'

'Still no good – wouldn't he have to be already in the

system for us to find a match?' Julius pointed out and they all looked at Reilly for affirmation.

'Correct. So again we're only talking about comparative evidence. All of your suggestions are great, and would certainly help mount a case against this guy if or when he's caught, but in the meantime, how do we help *catch* him? Come on, surely there's something among all this?'

The set of faces before her looked blank as they each raked through the evidence, and took yet another look at photographs of the scene.

Deciding to put them out of their misery, Reilly picked up the bagged burger.

'You were half right, Lucy,' she announced, holding it aloft. 'This is the single most important piece of evidence relating to this case. Not as Lucy pointed out, for DNA collection – although of course that too is important – but mostly because this innocent-looking cheeseburger can give us lots of information about this guy. His height, facial appearance, right down to whether he snores in bed or snuffles when he's awake.'

They looked at her, puzzled.

'In fact,' Reilly went on, studying the bag more closely, 'I can tell from just looking at it that our guy has got a thin, pinched face ... probably narrow too. And he seems to be missing a couple of wisdom teeth—'

'His bite mark,' Julius muttered, the penny finally dropping.

'Exactly. Now, a forensic dentist would have to give us specifics, but when time is of the essence and the cops are sure their attacker was the one eating the cheeseburger, we can at least confirm that it's a guy with a long, narrow face.'

Rory shook his head in wonderment. 'I would never have thought of that,' he admitted.

'Well,' the department's new specialist forensic investigator said with a smile, 'by the time I'm finished with you guys, there's nothing in this world you won't think of.'

2

At Harcourt Street station, Chris Delaney was putting the finishing touches to a written report when it happened again.

At first he tried to ignore it, putting the faint but all-too-familiar tingle in the joints of his first two fingers down to repetitive strain or sheer tiredness – he hadn't been to bed in over twenty-eight hours so it was only to be expected that his joints would be fatigued. He shook his hand to try and shake the pain, carefully turned the page on his report, put it neatly on the pile of finished papers, and picked up his pen again.

But then, as if to prove him wrong, the throbbing surged from his fingers through his left arm and upper body, almost sending him into spasm. Dropping the pen, Chris winced as the ache overwhelmed him, and when Pete Kennedy approached his desk, he struggled to remain impassive.

'What's up with you?' his fellow detective asked, eyebrows raised.

He tried to ride it out. 'Nothing, just got cramp – from all this bloody writing, probably,' he said through gritted teeth.

'Writing?' Kennedy sniffed, unconvinced. 'From all that pumping iron if you ask me. I don't know why the hell you bother.'

Although Kennedy was a towering six-footer and well able to carry some additional weight, he still had a bit of a paunch, something he had no interest in doing anything about. Chris, on the other hand, enjoyed his regular work-outs at the gym. It helped him cope with the demands of the job and he welcomed the physical endurance aspect too.

Based out of the Serious Crime Unit, he and Kennedy spent the majority of their time working city homicide. For a country that barely ten years ago reported one incident of murder every few months, the newer, affluent and decidedly more bloodthirsty citizens of Ireland seemed intent on making up for lost time. And as resources in their division were gradually becoming more and more stretched, things seemed to be getting progressively worse. Their latest case was an especially puzzling one.

A week earlier, a headless and dismembered male torso was found floating in the city's Royal Canal by a man out walking his dog. The Sub-Aqua Squad had spent hours in the murky, heavily polluted waters searching for remaining body parts and forensic evidence but so far had found nothing. Until they did, it was virtually impossible to identify the victim.

Following recent, similar episodic killings associated with sections of Ireland's growing ethnic communities, it was tempting for the authorities to explain it away as yet another ritualistic killing and while the murder certainly bore some of the hallmarks – such as dismemberment – Chris wasn't convinced. Some more sensationalist sections of the Irish media were only too eager to pin the incident on immigrants, but for him there was nothing definitive in the evidence so far that pointed the finger at any particular group. Not until they found the head, at any rate.

He swivelled round in his chair and looked at his watch. 'Well, seeing as all's quiet at the moment,' he said to Kennedy, 'I might head home for a few hours this morning – try and grab some sleep.'

He stacked his papers in a neat pile and put the pen away in his drawer, the thought of a couple of hours sleep sounding tempting. Not that it would make a blind bit of difference to his now almost continuous fatigue. Maybe he should pick up some of those multivitamin things on the way home – seeing that he hadn't been eating properly, something like that might make the difference. And if it didn't, well, then he'd have to think about getting himself checked out properly. He ruffled his dark hair in a desperate attempt to rouse himself. Not to mention organize a bloody long-overdue haircut.

'Detectives?'

Chris was already slipping his jacket on when one of

the uniforms put his head around the door, his tone agitated.

'What's up?' Kennedy growled from the depths of a bacon sandwich.

'O'Brien wants you both next door for a briefing – right away,' the uniform told them. 'And he looks pissed off.'

Chris and Kennedy exchanged looks. So much for sleep.

'What's it about?' Kennedy asked as they followed the younger man down the hallway toward the Inspector's office.

The uniform shrugged. 'Not a clue.'

Kennedy looked at Chris and winked. 'Let me guess – the Sub-Aqua Squad finally found that poor bastard's flute.'

O'Brien's office was a mess of papers, boxes of files stacked against the walls, folders strewn all across his desk. But the Inspector himself was sharp, his round, red face and flyaway gray hair notwithstanding.

'I wish it was something on the floater,' he muttered. 'But it's something else entirely.' His expression was grim. 'Double shooting, possible homicide/suicide south of the city, in Dalkey. One male, one female, both pronounced dead at the scene.'

'Domestic?'

'Unlikely. They're only kids, college kids, the girl barely in her twenties, apparently.' He ran his fingers through his hair, messing it up even more.

'Shit.' Kennedy shook his head.

'Too bloody right.' The Inspector leaned back in his

chair, looking like a man with the weight of the world on his shoulders.

'In Dalkey, you said?' Chris was taken aback at the victims' age and profile. Dalkey was a decidedly upmarket part of the city and shootings were an unusual occurrence.

'Maybe they stumbled across Daddy's hunting gun?' Kennedy said, evidently on a similar train of thought.

'Could be. I don't know what the weapon of choice was; to be honest, I don't know that much at all,' O'Brien replied. 'There's a unit from Blackrock already down there; they were first on the scene and as far as I know the Technical Bur—' He paused mid-sentence, and rolled his eyes. 'Sorry, I mean the *GFU* should be there by now too. It will take a bit of getting used to that one, although at least it rolls off the tongue a bit easier. Anyway, I need you two to get over there and see what you can make of it.' He shook his head. 'First the gangs, then the foreigners, and now we have posh kids shooting one another too – I'm telling you, this country's gone mad altogether.'

Chris steered the unmarked Ford toward a vacant parking space and looked up at the modern apartment block. Limestone walls, aluminium balconies, well-tended gardens, sea views ... Whoever owned this place had money.

'That's a hell of a vista,' he observed. Even in winter, the view out across Dublin Bay was spectacular, the rolling gray waves stacking up one by one as though impatient to crash against the shore.

'Hell of a turnout too,' Kennedy said, indicating the

mass of vehicles parked outside. 'I wonder would there be the same interest if the crime scene was on Sheriff Street?'

'Guess not, but there are some pretty powerful neighbors around here who need reassuring things are under control,' Chris replied, looking up the hill in the direction of Killiney, Dublin's own Beverly Hills.

'So, I wonder what kind of mood Miss America will be in today?' Kennedy mumbled, nodding toward Reilly Steel's GFU van. He lit a cigarette and leaned on the bonnet of the car, admiring the surroundings. Chris climbed from the car, trying not to groan at the ache in his legs. 'No point rushing in if she's still there. What do you make of her?' Kennedy asked.

Chris shrugged. 'Too early to say.'

'Oh come on – don't give me that. An FBI-trained crime tech brought over here to bring us country bumpkins up to date and you don't have an opinion?'

It was true that eyebrows had been raised at the appointment and when a photograph of the blond, blue-eyed American had been passed around, there had been some sceptical comments. But far from being a wide-eyed bimbo, the latest addition to the force had trained at the FBI facility at Quantico and had expert knowledge and considerable field experience, as well as valuable exposure to the workings of the institution's state-of-the-art crime lab. Steel had also apparently worked with some of the best forensic investigators in the world and was held in high regard by her peers. How the hell she had been lured to Dublin, Chris didn't know, but either way, he was glad to have someone with her credentials on board.

He waved a hand as Kennedy's smoke drifted toward him. 'I reckon the head brass knew what they were doing when they brought her in – the old Technical Bureau was thirty years behind the times and we need all the help we can get.'

Up until then, they'd had little to do with the American. She tended to stay in the lab, apparently preferring working on the evidence than working the scene – something Chris could certainly relate to. But today Steel had had no choice but to attend as Jack Gorman, the field investigator their unit normally worked with, was away on a Caribbean cruise with his wife – some big anniversary celebration apparently.

'Come on, let's go,' he said, starting toward the building.

His partner stubbed his cigarette out on the ground and heaved himself up off the bonnet.

Going inside, they headed for the fourth floor, Kennedy huffing and puffing all the way. A uniformed officer guarding the scene directed them to the bedroom where the shooting had taken place.

'Ah, hell,' Kennedy whispered as he entered the room.

The place was beautiful; a neutral color scheme, beige carpet and white walls, light-colored bed linen, and tall bay windows opening out to a stunning view of the bay – in fact everything was idyllic except for the crimson blood splattered across the bed and up the wall.

The victims lay together on the bed, both fully naked. The girl's eyes were closed, her dark hair fanned out prettily on the pillow, looking for all the world as though she was having a post-coital nap – apart from the gaping hole low in her chest and half the contents of her companion's head sprayed across her cheek.

They were achingly young, in their early-twenties at the most. Chris's stomach turned over. Their boss was right – what kind of country was it that a kid barely out of his teens could get his hands on a gun? And a posh kid at that. Judging by his lightly tanned skin and toned rugby-player physique, he suspected that the boyfriend wasn't some malnourished scumbag the girl had taken up with to piss off her well-to-do parents. And he had one of those stylized oriental tattoos on his upper right arm, not the Celtic cross favored by the working classes.

His eyes quickly scanned the area. The murder weapon lay on the sheets – a 9 mm. It must have fallen out of the shooter's hand.

He briefly exchanged nods with state pathologist, who was conducting her preliminary examination of the bodies before their removal to the morgue. He gave an involuntary shiver. Sometimes Karen Thompson unsettled him more than the victims did. A serious woman with oversized dark eyes, Roman nose, and an exceptionally long neck, Chris figured she was perfectly suited for the strain of medicine where the absence of a bedside manner was a good thing. Briefly noting the arrival of the detectives, she resumed her examination of the bodies.

Several uniforms were busy around the apartment, some taking notes, most simply observing and helping guard the scene – a crime like this always drew a crowd. The GFU crew, dressed head to toe in white dust suits, were wandering around the area; dusting for prints on surfaces, gathering material and trace evidence, bagging everything as they went.

One of the forensics squatted low against the bed as he pointed and flashed his camera at the victims. And although he hadn't yet spotted Reilly Steel, Chris knew she had to be somewhere amongst the mix.

'Christ,' Kennedy muttered. 'What age were these two – fifteen?'

'College students according to Reilly, so they've got to be older than that.'

'But not by much. Bloody hell.'

Although in the course of their work they came across young victims on a regular basis, they were usually junkies or fledgling gang members who'd come from such troubled backgrounds it was almost impossible to imagine them ending up any other way. These kids, though – healthy, educated, middle class – could just as easily have been Kennedy's own nephew or daughter and for those reasons alone, it made it different.

'What the hell was he thinking?'

'Where the hell did he get the gun is what I want to know,' Chris ruminated.

Illegal weapons were increasingly finding their way out of the hands of paramilitaries and onto the city streets and, while any criminal worth his salt would know how to get hold of a gun at short notice, it should be a different story for a middle-class college kid.

He turned to the uniformed officer standing in the bedroom doorway. 'Who was first on the scene?'

'A unit from Blackrock,' the man replied, indicating a group of officers gathered in the living room – one of them decidedly shaky-looking. 'Young Fitzgerald is not long out of training,' he added with a slight shake of the head. 'Talk about throwing him in at the deep end.'

Chris cursed inwardly. He'd spotted Fitzgerald as soon as he'd stepped into the living room – he looked as young as the victims, he'd probably only just started shaving.

He stepped into the living room. Like the bedroom, it had tall French windows opening out onto a balcony with a sea view. A massive plasma TV screen filled one wall and a deep fireplace dominated the other. The whole place smelled of money. Chris wondered if there had been a robbery of some kind, but judging by the valuable objects scattered around the place, they obviously hadn't taken much.

He called the rookie over, who marched up to the two detectives, snapped to attention and straightened his uniform.

'Officer Fitzgerald,' Kennedy began, 'take your time and tell us what you can remember.'

Somewhat surprisingly, the younger cop was calm and articulate as he outlined what had happened when he first reached the apartment. 'The 999 was logged at 6.03 a.m. from this building, apparently by another resident who'd heard a gunshot coming from the apartment,' he informed the detectives.

'OK.'

'Our unit responded quickly,' he continued, 'and arrived at the scene at precisely 6.18 a.m.'

'Six-eighteen a.m. precisely?' Chris echoed, amused by the young man's certainty.

'Precisely, sir. I checked my watch just to be sure.'

The detectives exchanged a surreptitious look. 'All right. And then?'

'Well, at first we were ordered not to penetrate the building in case the perpetrator was still at large.'

Despite himself, Chris was tickled by the younger officer's terminology – it was something the training colleges instilled with vigour into new recruits. Personally, he wasn't a fan of this 'Robocop' talk and whenever he gave a radio or TV statement, he purposely spoke in layman's terms so the public could be assured that if they did come forward with information, someone in the force might actually be capable of understanding them.

'Then, at 6.45, we got word that the building was secure and they gave us the OK to go in,' Fitzgerald continued. 'So in we went.'

'Please tell me you didn't use the lift to get up here,' Kennedy remarked.

Looking faintly hurt, Fitzgerald shook his head. 'Of course not. The perpetrator may have used the elevators, so we made sure we entered via the stairs in order to avoid contaminating evidence.' He paused. 'I might be new, but I'm not stupid, Detective,' he added, pointedly.

Chris had begun to draw the exact same conclusion. 'So this is how you found them.'

'Yes, sir. It was obvious as soon as we arrived that both victims were dead, so we called it in as a homicide and possible suicide and made sure not to touch a thing until the forensic people got here.' He added the last part with emphasis, looking directly at Kennedy.

The kid could stand up for himself. Chris was impressed.

'Did you find out who called in the 999?' Chris asked.

Fitzgerald nodded and flipped open a black notebook. 'The woman living in the apartment next door, a Mrs Maura McKenna. Now, she doesn't remember everything exactly as it happened.' He sounded vaguely disappointed that his only witness wasn't up to his own high standards. 'According to her statement, she was fast asleep in bed when she heard a sound that quote – nearly lifted her out of her skin – unquote,' he said, reading from the notebook. 'The second shot came soon after, although she's unable to remember exactly how soon, but she believes it could have been four or five minutes. Then she rang 999.'

'OK.'

'She was also able to give us a possible ID on one of the victims. The girl living here is – or rather, *was* – Clare Ryan. She's a student at UCD. The old lady said that the girl's parents bought this apartment for her a couple of years back, when she first started at university. She doesn't know anything about a boyfriend, though.'

'Anything else?'

'That's it, sir,' the younger man said in conclusion.

'Thanks, we'll have a chat with the neighbor later,' Chris said, dismissing him.

Just a quick scan of the room confirmed that the dead girl was indeed Clare Ryan – there was a long white sideboard in the living room dotted with framed photographs of a smiling brunette. Chris picked up a photo, taken on a beach somewhere – Thailand, maybe? The sand was pure white, the sea azure. The girl's happy grin and lively eyes were a sad and stark contrast to the pale, lifeless cadaver in the bedroom.

'Any photos of the guy?' He looked up from his reverie and saw Kennedy watching him.

His gaze scanned the photographs for any sign of her companion. 'Who can tell?'

It was difficult to match any of the males in the photos to the dead guy, given that most of his head had been obliterated.

Kennedy studied the photos with him. 'Once her ID is confirmed, it should make it easier to identify the boyfriend – he was probably a student too.' He wandered over to the window, gazed out across the bay. 'Who'd buy a college kid a swanky place like this?'

'Good investment for the parents and they know their kid is living somewhere safe – or at least that's what they would have hoped.'

He and Kennedy would need to talk to Clare Ryan's college friends and fellow students. Hopefully they'd be able to shed some light on who the guy was and maybe why he had done what he did. The obvious theory was that he was the jealous type. Clare had been a good-looking girl, that much was evident from the photographs. Slim, with big brown eyes and an engaging smile, chances were the pretty brunette had turned more than a few heads on campus and that might have pissed off Prince Charming.

Or perhaps he'd been a previous Prince Charming and

the guy had taken the break-up very badly. There were a few scenarios but no point in surmising at this stage, Chris thought, at least not until they found out more about Clare Ryan and her dead companion.

The detectives headed back toward the bedroom, but found their passage blocked by one of the uniforms.

'Sorry, I can't let you in,' the officer said, his tone apologetic. 'No one's allowed in for the moment.'

'What?' Kennedy frowned. 'What are you talking about? Of course we're going in.'

The officer looked uncomfortable. 'There's nothing I can do for the minute,' he said, giving a quick glance over his shoulder. 'She'll murder me.'

'Who will?' Chris asked. 'Dr Thompson? She should be finished by now – she was almost done when I saw her a few minutes ago.'

'No, not her,' the uniform answered, 'that new one from the crime lab – the American. She ordered everyone out and warned me not to let anyone into the room until she's finished.'

'Finished doing what?' Kennedy asked, straining to see past him. Then his eyes widened as he caught sight of something through the doorway. 'What the hell?' he spat, turning to Chris in astonishment.

They peered inside. Reilly Steel was standing in the middle of the bedroom with her eyes closed and her arms wide open.

'Looks like she's doing some kind of yoga chant or something,' Kennedy snorted in derision.

'That's not it,' said a young female crime tech standing

nearby. Her voice dropped to a whisper. 'She does this all the time, draws on her instincts, uses her senses to see if she can recreate the scene in her mind.' As she spoke, there was admiration in her voice.

'Touchy-feely crap,' Kennedy rolled his eyes.

'I don't think it *is* actually, Detective,' the woman replied. 'In the States her solve-assist rate was over 80 per cent.'

Chris had read this somewhere too. While Reilly Steel evidently had some unorthodox methods, her investigative record spoke for itself. Still, he thought with a grin, there was no getting away from the fact that this 'touchy-feely crap' would raise a few eyebrows in this neck in the woods, and it clearly wasn't going down too well with Kennedy.

'Yeah, well,' his partner muttered, 'if she thinks the rest of us are going to *sniff* our way through this investigation, she's got another bloody think coming.'

'I wouldn't dream of it,' a female voice replied from behind him. 'Besides, I doubt that whiskey nose of yours can detect much these days.'

Realizing that Steel had left the bedroom and overheard him, Kennedy's neck reddened and his face instantly turned a brighter shade of puce.

'Yeah, well ... we couldn't get in ...' he babbled.

'Sorry about that,' she said, extending a hand. 'Reilly Steel, GFU. I take it you're the assigned detective?'

'We both are,' Chris replied. 'This is Pete Kennedy and I'm Chris Delaney. Pleased to meet you.'

'Pleasure,' she said with a bright smile.

OK, Chris thought, so he'd seen the press release

photos and heard all the blond jokes but bloody hell ...
Considering her unglamorous occupation, Reilly Steel was
a stunner. Her huge sea-blue eyes shone with a bright
intensity and her lightly bronzed skin stood out in marked
contrast to the white clinical cap she was wearing. Beneath
it, he knew there was a mane of honey-blond hair, but
despite her obvious beauty, or perhaps because of it, he
could tell instantly that she was sharp and
uncompromising.

'Well, I've pretty much finished my erm ... touchy-feely
stuff,' she said, a glint of amusement in her eye, 'and the
ME's done her thing, but we've still got a bit of work to do
in there.' She moved back to the bedroom. 'You guys can
come in – as long as you don't get in my way,' she added,
looking sideways at Kennedy.

'No problem.' The older detective remained uncharac-
teristically muted as they followed her back inside.

'Have you found anything out of the ordinary?' Chris
asked.

She moved to the foot of the bed. 'We won't know for
sure until autopsy, but judging by the entry wound ...' she
indicated Clare Ryan, whose body was now being carefully
zipped into a black polythene body bag, '... the girl was
shot in the chest from less than two feet. Point-blank
range.'

She moved around, re-enacting the crime as she did. 'It
looks like he was standing at the foot of the bed when he
fired the first shot, then lay down beside her before
finishing himself off. Chances are she was still breathing at
the time.'

Chris agreed. The amount of blood that had pooled beneath the girl suggested that she hadn't died instantly. 'He seemed to do a much better job on himself, though,' he added, his tone grim as he glanced at what was left of the young man's head. 'Not exactly Romeo and Juliet.'

'No.' Reilly bent down and picked up her forensic toolbox. 'We'll do a tox screen on the blood – see if it's a case of a trip gone bad or something.'

'Thanks, we'd be grateful for anything you could give us,' he said, ignoring Kennedy's disapproving gaze. His partner – like much of the force – was still largely sceptical about forensics, preferring instead to rely on good old-fashioned detective work and let the lab people back up *their* findings instead of the other way round.

'Chances are it's drug related, though. What isn't these days?' Kennedy grumbled.

'Well, I'd rather reserve judgement until we know more,' Reilly replied. 'I'll take a closer look at what we've got when we get back to the lab, though I'll be honest, it doesn't seem to be all that much. Of course, we've got a couple of cartridges to process, along with the weapon. Speaking of which ...' She snapped on a fresh pair of latex gloves and moved toward the gun, which could be safely retrieved now that the victims' bodies had been removed.

A gaggle of police officers had gathered in the room, grateful for the chance to be around something more interesting. Bit by bit, the majority had drifted back in once the pathologist had left and the victims' bodies were removed.

'Hey, can you guys stand back and give me some room?' Reilly asked, impatiently.

Realizing what she was about to do, Fitzgerald, the younger officer with whom the detectives had spoken earlier, quickly reached inside his pocket. 'Here,' he said, proudly presenting a pencil to her, 'you'll need this.'

Kennedy chuckled. 'What? Is she supposed to draw a picture of it or something?'

The younger man looked at him blankly. 'But don't you have to pick up the gun without handling it?' he asked, no longer quite so confident. 'In order to ... you know ... protect fingerprints and that?'

'You've been watching way too much TV,' Reilly said indulgently, taking the pencil and putting it aside. 'If I used your pencil to pick it up, I might disturb any gunpowder deposits or dirt lodged in the barrel. Dislodged dirt could alter striation markings on test-fired bullets and we don't want to do that, do we?' she added, in the manner of someone speaking to a 5-year-old.

'Um, no, I suppose not.' Fitzgerald looked almost sorry he'd asked.

'But you're right, of course, we *are* worried about protecting prints,' she went on, beckoning him forward to observe what she was doing, while the others kept out of her way. She knelt down by the bed and indicated for the officer to kneel beside her. 'But if I hold the weapon there,' she pointed to the butt of the gun, 'see the chequered part of the grip?' The rookie nodded, his attention firmly fixed on the weapon. 'Now, this part has such an uneven striation that it won't retain any identifiable prints, so it's fine to handle it here. Not to mention that it's the safest way to do it – I don't want the damn thing to accidentally discharge on me, either.' She slowly and cautiously lifted the gun up off the bed. Lesson over, she beckoned one of the others to help her safely prepare the gun for processing.

Fitzgerald looked at Reilly Steel with something approaching pure adoration. Chris smiled. Whatever the older guys in the force might think, the latest member of the GFU clearly had a set of fans amongst the younger generation.

3

Reilly sat at her desk, her features screwed up in an expression of intense concentration as she studied the crime-scene inventory for the Clare Ryan case. It was a couple of days after the shooting and nearly all the staff had long since left for the day.

To most people, the clinical setting and the oppressive silence – broken only by the low hum of the machinery – would feel eerie and discomfiting. For Reilly, however, the peace and quiet of late evening was her preferred time to work.

Now that everyone had gone home, she was free from the noisy distractions of twenty or so laboratory staff laboring all around her. The silence allowed her more time to work, more time to think, and tonight it might allow her uncover what it was about this shooting that had been niggling at her for the last two days.

She'd sensed from the start that something wasn't right

but so far had found nothing out of the ordinary amongst the evidence to back this feeling up. The two things she trusted most during an investigation were evidence and instinct. And since leaving that scene, Reilly's instincts were screaming that something was seriously amiss.

Gorman would have laughed if she'd tried to explain this to him. The long-time incumbent, he was head of the old forensic department and hadn't exactly been over the moon about her appointment, or the setting up of the new unit in general. She was glad that the old man would be away on vacation for a while; it gave her an opportunity to run this case the way she wanted – the way she was trained to do back home.

Since she'd arrived at the GFU, he'd tried to put her in her place, inferring that her job was just to oversee work in the lab, and that she should have little or no interference in what he was doing, or had done, up to now. While this was true to a degree, from what Reilly had seen, the older man's current methods were pretty half-hearted and pedantic considering it was such an important role, and the old dog had no interest in new tricks.

On top of it, Gorman had an unbelievable ego – something she'd at least been forewarned about before she got here. Like many traditional scientists, he seemed to operate under the belief that his word was gospel and he was also a condescending old chauvinist – something she could handle were he not such a sloppy investigator with it. Still she resented the way he spoke to the female staff, particularly Lucy, who was a real sweetie and Reilly knew was routinely wounded by her superior's dismissiveness.

But, office politics aside, Reilly also had to deal with the force's natural resistance to an 'outsider', to say nothing of the inevitable dumb blond jokes. She shook her head, recalling how, on her very first day at the office, she'd come out of a morning meeting to find a crimson Baywatch-style swimsuit laid out on her desk. No doubt the culprit and his buddies found it hilarious but it was water off a duck's back to Reilly; she'd had to deal with a lot worse back in her FBI student days.

She looked again at the evidence for the Ryan homicide. This was one of the first scenes she'd managed to coordinate entirely on her own, outside of Gorman's interference. Without him breathing down her neck, she'd had as much time as she wanted to run the scene in as much detail as possible. And plenty of time to apply her 'touchy-feely' techniques, she thought, biting back a smile as she recalled the reaction *that* had gotten.

It was something she'd learned and perfected at Quantico. Her lecturer, Rob Crichton, one of the best forensic investigators in the business, had drilled into his recruits the importance of the three-dimensional crime scene. She smiled fondly, recalling the now deceased Crichton – an anti-personnel device at a perp's apartment having put an end to the life of one of the best criminalists she'd ever had the fortune to work with. Although his death was a tragedy, she figured that Rob would have appreciated the irony of his body being blown to smithereens. He himself finally becoming the physical evidence he'd spent much of his life collecting.

'Your senses are there for a reason, people,' he used to say. 'Never, *ever* discount them.'

While Reilly had initially been sceptical, she soon discovered when she applied Rob's painstaking methods that she had an unusually keen sense of smell – something that had been invaluable in almost every case she worked. For some reason, she was particularly attuned to perfume and could draw easily on her inner database of various fragrance brands and body creams. For example, she knew that the ME, Karen Thompson, favored Red Door by Elizabeth Arden, and that Carol, the GFU receptionist, routinely wore CK One. Oddly, she'd noticed that Chanel No. 5, the American woman's favourite had a far less fervent following on this side of the Atlantic.

Either way, her instincts had served her well in the past and she wasn't about to discard them just because some red-nosed Irish cop thought they were dumb and irrelevant. All mouth and little substance; Reilly could eat a guy like Kennedy for breakfast – not that she wanted to, she thought, shuddering at the notion. He seemed OK, just old school. She'd heard his partner's name mentioned a few times over the last couple of months; Chris Delaney seemed to have a good reputation within the force, and unlike some of his more conservative colleagues, also seemed to be well disposed toward the GFU. She figured that those dark, almost Mediterranean looks must work well when it came to extracting information – particular from the female side of the population – although from what little she knew about him, he didn't seem the type to play on that. And in contrast to Kennedy, he certainly hadn't given her any attitude that morning, and seemed happy to take on board anything significant the lab might come up with.

Which, at the moment, wasn't exactly much.

They'd sent blood samples off for a toxicology screen which, if they came back positive, might – for the shooter at least – go some way toward explaining his actions. However, with the speed the labs worked at, who knew when she'd get those back.

They'd also collected the usual – fingerprints, trace, and fibers – which were now being analyzed. Ballistics were in possession of the gun and cartridges, and Reilly was planning on calling down there the following morning to see if they'd come up with anything of interest.

In the meantime, she was doing what she did best, going over the scene in her mind, trying to recreate the kill, taking into account the evidence they'd uncovered, and hoping for something, anything, that might just help move this case forward.

But so far, all Reilly could come up with was that something didn't feel right.

She sat forward in her seat and for the umpteenth time picked up the photos of the victims taken at the scene before their removal. Again, she studied the blood and brain spatter on the headboard; much of the gray matter had spewed over the dead girl's face and hair – some even landing as far away as the pile of books on her bedside table. The blowback blood droplets on the headboard and wall behind were to be expected, traveling in the opposite direction to the path of the bullet. Her gaze moved downward to the gun's resting position on the bed where it had ended up after falling out of the dead shooter's hand.

What was it? she thought, kneading her forehead in the vain hope that the answer might somehow be released. What was it that about this whole situation that was bothering her? Given the gun's caliber, trajectory and shooting distance, as well as the residue found on the guy's hand, the results all looked consistent, yet there was something telling her that there was more to this, that she was missing something. Something important.

But what?

Chasing evidence, hoping to find answers – sometimes Reilly felt it was all she'd been doing her whole life.

End of excerpt

Continue reading TABOO, or download the CSI Reilly Steel Boxset & save 50%

ABOUT THE AUTHOR

Casey Hill is the pseudonym of husband and wife writing team, Kevin and Melissa Hill. They live in Dublin, Ireland. TABOO, the first title in a series of forensic thrillers featuring Californian-born CSI Reilly Steel was an international bestseller upon release. It was followed by subsequent books, INFERNO (aka TORN) HIDDEN, THE WATCHED & TRACE. A prequel to the series CRIME SCENE, is also available.

Translation rights to the series have been sold in multiple languages including Russian, Turkish and Japanese.

Subscribe to the mailing list. Enter the following link into your browser to be notified of new Casey Hill releases: http://eepurl.com/FFE2D

caseyhillbooks.com
info@caseyhillbooks.com

ALSO BY CASEY HILL

Author Page

CPSIA information can be obtained
at www.ICGtesting.com
Printed in the USA
BVHW031837250319
543646BV00001B/136/P